JAKE/GEEK

JAKE/GEEK

Quest for Oshi

Reonne Haslett

Published by Expansive Press

Edited by Deborah Vetter
Cover art by Chinthaka Pradeep
Book design and layout by Christy Collins, Constellation Book Design
Hacked font created by David Libeau

ISBN (paperback): 978-1-7370573-0-7
ISBN (ebook): 978-1-7370573-1-4

Printed in the United States of America

CHAPTER 1
BOY WONDER

When it comes to computers, I'm a genius. When it comes to girls, I'm lost. My reputation as a geek at Palo Alto High doesn't hurt my girl radar, but with so many in my orbit, who do I go and fall for? My best friend. I'm pathetic. My name is Jake Green, and I've known Oshi O'Malley forever, maybe even in a past life or in another galaxy. Who knows, but no one gets me like her. And now... I'm going to ruin it.

The first bell rings. I dawdle in the hallway, hoping to run into Oshi. Every year, when lockers are assigned, we arrange to be next to each other. They're like our touchstone. The second bell rings and Oshi hasn't shown up. I'm more disappointed than I should be. And then, I smell her fresh lavender scent.

"Hey, Greenie." Oshi brushes past me as she comes around the corner. The activities of the outside world carry on—metal clanging, feet shuffling, teens tussling—but my world stops. I'm caught in her vortex.

"Going to geek club?" she asks, poking around in her locker.

I stare at the back of her head, waiting for my brain synapses to fire. "Yeah," I finally sputter. Fortunately, she doesn't seem to notice, or if she does, she's sparing me.

She turns, long black hair swaying like silk in a soft breeze. "We should study for that comp sci test," she says. Briefly, her dark eyes stare into my core, and then she's gone, lost in a sea of students, leaving me in a sea of doubt.

When did things become so awkward with Oshi? I feel like the biggest fool on the planet. I mean, we grew up together. When we were four we stuck beans up our noses. At five we got time-outs for stealing her mom's fresh-baked cupcakes. Started a neighborhood club and sold lemonade on the curb at seven. Our families spend every Christmas, Halloween, and 4th of July together. We played pranks on our siblings, broke-in video games, rode the scariest carnival rides, scuba-dived and rock-climbed on family vacations, snuggled close during thunderstorms, and cried on each other's shoulder whenever we were hurt. What is happening to me? Heart fluttering, gut clenching, sweat producing feelings, I don't want.

I arrive at the computer lab at 2:35pm exactly. Students are crammed into cubicles. My eyes search the room, and they find her, deep in conversation with Sean Haggerty, wannabe rock star. I don't know if there are hairs on the back of my neck, but if there are, they must be standing up. He's hanging over her cubicle, all six feet of him. Who gets to be six feet tall by the time they are a junior? Oh, and did I mention that he's dark and handsome, too?

I don't believe those adjectives have ever been applied to me. I'm tall, like my father, and probably too skinny. If my body got as many workouts as my mind, I might be in shape. As it is, I've heard the word "gangly" when people didn't know I was listening. Shaggy brown hair hangs in my eyes which my mom says are the color of the Mediterranean Sea. Until recently, I've not given much thought to what the opposite sex thinks of me. Now, I smooth my hair with my hands before I approach Oshi's cubicle.

Sean notices me first. Is it my imagination, or is his eye-tooth sparkling like Dastardly Whiplash from that old cartoon, Rocky and Bullwinkle? I want to rush over and rescue Oshi from the railroad tracks, but instead, I saunter. When I reach them, the villain addresses me, "What's up, Green?"

"Not much," I reply, eyes on Oshi.

She looks up. "Hey Greenie...ready to study?"

Sean chimes in, sarcasm dripping like syrup, "Yeah, better hit the books...*Greenie.*" He draws this last part out. I refuse to look at him. I don't want him to see that he's getting under my skin.

Oshi touches Sean's arm and gazes up at him. "I'll see you at band practice tonight," she says. I stare, transfixed.

I can feel Sean watching me for a reaction. When he gets none, he stretches instead, revealing pumped biceps and a six-pack. "Yeah, sure, see ya tonight." He winks at *me.* My inner ninja wants to give him a swift kick to the groin. I let that impulse go and stumble into a chair next to Oshi. My chest feels tight, and my palms are sweaty as I take out my book.

Sean leaves and I inquire, "Band practice?"

Oshi's never played an instrument in her life, although I rarely see her without headphones in. She loves music and always sings along.

"Sweet, huh?" she answers, shifting in her chair to face me. She seems completely oblivious to the beads of sweat on my brow and the tremor in my hands. "He invited me to join his band. He thinks I have a great voice."

Yeah, I'll bet he does, I think, but don't say. Instead, I snigger. She pokes my arm, hard. "What?"

I'd do anything to reverse time. "Nothing, I...just..." *Come on, wonder boy, recovery necessary.* "It's just...I didn't know you wanted to sing in a band." A lame smile forms on my face.

Oshi is gentle with me. "Really? Don't you remember when our moms put us in the church choir when we were seven? I've always loved to sing."

"Oh, yeah," I fumble. "You were really good in that choir!" *I'm an idiot.*

She laughs out loud, then puts her eraser to her lips. I watch, maybe a bit too closely. "Yeah, we have a gig Saturday night at The Garage," she says. "I'm really nervous. I mean, they say it gets really crowded. It would be great if you could be there, Greenie."

"Sure," I answer indifferently, knowing an army of poison dart frogs couldn't keep me away.

She opens her binder. "We better get started or we'll be here till midnight." My heart flips at the prospect, even though I know she's not serious.

We make an honorable attempt at studying, which is no simple task for Oshi and me. Throw any arbitrary subject at us, and we can chat for hours, but cramming for a test makes us choke. We continually remind each other to focus.

Finally, Oshi says, "I've got to get home for dinner, then to Sean's for practice. He's going to teach me my lyrics," she says. I gulp, then nod and help her pack her stuff. "Thanks. See ya tomorrow." She gives me a friendly squeeze. My eyes stay glued on her until every limb has cleared the doorway. After Oshi leaves, I remain in the lab, as usual. Rodrigo, the janitor, lets me hang out until he locks up at six. I wonder what he thinks of me, the nerdy kid staying so late. "Why doesn't this kid get a life?" or "Doesn't this kid have a home?" I have a life and a home, but the less he knows about them the better.

Blame it on the genes. I didn't grow up the offspring of Justin Green, legendary computer scientist, without techie cells coursing through my veins. Like a vampire lusting for blood, I lust for code. By the time I was ten, I had mastered every computer game I could get my hands on. Other dads might teach their sons how to throw a football, mine taught me JavaScript.

I programmed my first game, *Genius Toads*, when I was eleven. Dad tried selling it to a game publisher, but they said the graphics were mediocre. I honed my skills and programmed a new game, *Avenging Maniacs*. It has stellar graphics and difficult levels. Rather than selling it, we marketed it ourselves. At twelve years old, I became the CEO of my own company, Jake Green Games.

Two more games followed in two years: *Castle of Zombies* and *Fortress of Ninjas*. I wish I could say sales are making me rich, but that would mean I'm living in fantasyland. Most of the profits go into my college fund and the rest into my dad's bank account. It's not like he doesn't deserve it—without him there would be no Jake Green Games—it's just that he hassles me to develop new games, even though I don't want to do it anymore. Sometimes, when I'm angry, I want to scream, "Hey Pops, why don't you just stay employed for ten minutes and fill your own coffers." I keep my thoughts to myself though because I know I'd feel like a scumbag afterwards, considering his circumstances.

Lately, it seems Dad gets fired more than hired. I recently dropped by one of his consultancy jobs and was surprised to find his team drinking Frappuccinos and playing online poker. No one had heard from Dad in days, which they said was normal. Bracing myself for the worst, I went to his apartment. I found him stamping back and forth in smelly pajamas, his hair sticking up, á la Einstein, an Expo marker in one hand and a half-empty bottle of scotch in the other. Scribbled equations covered the walls. It looked fascinating, but taking the bottle away, and guiding him to the shower, was not.

Dad fits the high functioning autism profile. He likes to remind me that extreme intelligence can be associated with autism. Dad's a brilliant wizard, that's for sure. He's one of the innovators of much of the computer technology we take for granted. Computer scientists like my dad were behind the scenes at MIT, Harvard, Yale and Stanford in the 1980's, before laptops, smart phones and iPads. Some worked for the military. Their inventive minds, and the technology they developed, helped pave the way for many of today's internet tycoons.

Dad says that some historians believe Albert Einstein and Isaac Newton were autistic. He's always talking about famous geniuses who were on the spectrum, like John Forbes Nash Jr., the Princeton mathematician who was the subject of the film *A Beautiful Mind*; also Vincent van Gogh, the painter who cut off his own ear and allegedly died from a self-inflicted gunshot wound; and his favorite, Edgar Allan Poe, author of macabre stories like *The Pit and the Pendulum* and *The Tell-Tale Heart*. When someone asked Poe if he was insane, he answered the question with a question, "Is it madness, or the loftiest intelligence?"

The shrinks prescribe Dad medication, but the side effects make him miserable—headaches, restlessness, irritability. Like Beethoven, Hemingway and Churchill before him, Dad prefers to self-medicate with booze, and he's been getting worse since the divorce. Being the son of a famous, genius alcoholic isn't always easy. I'll take the lofty intelligence, but leave the madness, thank you.

I'm applying those genetic gifts here in the computer lab right now, but it's difficult to concentrate with Rodrigo whistling his upbeat Mexican tune.

"Uh, perdón?" I say in my best Spanish accent.

"¿Qué?" he responds.

"I'm trying to study here."

He goes back to sweeping. "Empollón," he mumbles. I Google the meaning: *Nerd*. Ignoring Rodrigo, I focus on what I do best, creating computer viruses.

CHAPTER 2
PINK HOME LIFE

Tall elm trees form an arch over our shady lane. It's a desirable neighborhood, close to Stanford University and the old downtown. This time of the evening I rarely see anyone, except maybe an eco-conscious professor on a bicycle. The neighbor's dog knocks over a trash can. I barely hear it. I'm listening to Spotify and fuming over Oshi at band practice with Sean. My mom's car is still in the driveway. I enter quietly because I want to get to my room before the inevitable encounter.

"Jake? Is that you?" My mom's voice calls from the deep recesses of our home.

"Who else?"

"Computer lab, again?" she asks, obvious irritation in her voice.

"Uh-huh."

"I wish you would have called. I have to go. Mrs. Bailey's baby is breech!"

"Whoa! Better hurry." I feign enthusiasm. I want her to think I care, but it probably doesn't matter anyway. She's distracted, as usual, focusing on getting to the hospital in time. Her record as an obstetrician is flawless; she's never missed a birth.

"Pizza's on the way. Money's in the cookie jar," she says, grabbing her keys.

"Thanks."

"Make sure your sister does her homework," she calls out, closing the front door.

My sister, Sara, comes out of her room. "Pizza again?" she complains. "I'm so sick of pizza I could puke."

What eleven-year-old kid doesn't like pizza? "Go do your homework," I say, hoping to deflect her. She sticks her tongue out and does an about-face.

During the divorce proceedings, the judge called us into her chambers separately. She gave us the choice of which parent we wanted to live with. We both chose our mother, Dr. Monica Green, aka Mumsy, an affectionate endearment which stuck when Sara couldn't get enough Scooby-Doo. Scooby-Doo fans may recall that Mumsy-Doo is Scooby-Doo's mother, and they all live on the Knittingham Puppy Farm.

It was a tad awkward that day, outside the judge's chambers. The conversation went something like:

Sara: "Who'd you pick?"

Jake: "Dad."

Sara: "Oh, whew."

Jake: "What's that supposed to mean?"

Sara: "I was scared you were gonna pick Mumsy."

Jake: "Well, actually, I did pick Mumsy, I was just B.S.ing you to see what you'd say."

Sara: (who at this point began punching me) "What? You shoulda picked Dad. I've searched the statistics—teenage boys are better off with their fathers." And on and on like that for ten minutes. She painted a pretty little picture of life with Mumsy, tucked away in the expensive tract home, with matching pink bedspread and curtains and no big brother to deal with. Sara and Mumsy, curled up on the couch together, munching pink popcorn and watching Scooby-Doo.

I had a different vision, and it did not include living with an alcoholic father in a tiny one-bedroom apartment five miles from school. Babysitting Sara sucks, but having the house to myself doesn't. Mumsy's dedication to her patients is renowned and her notoriety keeps her away from home more than the average parent. I'm lucky, I guess. All Mumsy requires from me is to babysit Sara, take out the garbage and stay out of trouble. It's an arrangement I can live with, and a heck of a lot better than having to parent a parent. Having a tech genius for a father gives me kudos with the geek squad, but I sometimes wonder what it would be like to have a dad who loves baseball and working out at the gym—not that I particularly like either of those. They say the apple doesn't fall far from the tree. I'm probably more like him—at the core—than I care to admit.

With Sara tucked neatly in her room, I can get back down to business. The KEEP OUT sign on my bedroom door says it all—do not enter my sacred space. One huge bonus of being Justin Green's kid is getting tons of computer stuff. Before my dad's colleagues introduce new products, they are tested by geeks who work out the kinks. I'm a hi-tech guinea pig.

Currently, I've got three gaming CPU's, two 40" monitors and a 60" monitor, five laptops in various stages of reconstruction and tablets from three different manufacturers. I've got apps coming out my ears. I need back-up drives to hold my back-up drives.

Once I run a program through the tests, I hack it for fun. About a year ago, I started messing around with coding viruses to destroy programs after I tested them. What a rush! When that got boring, I began putting viruses out on the net. I get to watch security companies try to crack my viral code. It's a risky chess game between me and the virus-busters. When I get the inevitable inkling of guilt, I quell it by telling myself that I'm gaining valuable experience. Too bad I can't include it on a resume. The thought makes me laugh out loud. I'm jolted out of my levity when Sara bangs on my bedroom door.

Irritation spikes my tone. "What?" I ask, flinging the door open.

Sara stands there, waving a mascara brush in my direction. "The pizza guy is here," she says, unaffected by my mood. A kaleidoscope of colorful make-up adorns her face, and she's wearing a costume that includes a fake fur wrap and a tutu.

"What the...?"

"I'm practicing lines for the play I wrote," she says. "I'm the lead, you know."

I shake my head and walk down the hall. The pizza guy is standing in the foyer, holding a plastic warming bag.

"Hold up, dude," I say as I go to the kitchen to grab the money from the cookie jar. Just as I'm exiting the kitchen, my phone beeps.

"Be right there," I yell to the pizza guy.

It's a text from Oshi: Band practice is amazing. Sean's so helpful. I love it!

I want to text back: *Why do you like that poser?*

Instead, I text: Great! Have fun!

The pizza guy waits in the foyer, holding up the pizza bag. His arms must be tired, and his logoed shirt and baseball cap really make him look like a goob. I feel sorry for him. I don't want to be in his shoes when I'm eighteen. He takes the medium pizza box out of its warmer and hands it to me. I give him thirty bucks. "I'll get your change," he says, reaching into his pocket.

"Keep it, man."

His eyes grow big. "No way," he says. "Seriously, dude? Thanks!"

"Whatevs," I say, to cover my embarrassment. "It's my mom's anyway."

He chuckles nervously, backing out the door. "Yeah, whatevs."

I don't know if I gave him the big tip because he looks like he could use it, or because, if I'm ever in his position, I'd want someone to do that for me.

Sara comes into the kitchen as I'm setting the box down on the counter, "Here ya' go. Try not to puke," I say, pushing past her.

"What's your problem?" she asks.

"Nothing," I say, but the truth is, my blood is boiling. I go to my room and slam the door. All I can think about is Oshi and Sean together. I pick up the old laptop I'm restoring and throw it across the room. *Ah, now that feels better.* Quickly an external hard drive follows, and before I know it, I'm in full-scale warfare mode, nothing safe from my rage. Who cares? There's more where that came from—one of the perks of being the fallen apple.

Sara bangs on my door, "Jake? Are you okay?"

"Oh, yes, darling sister," I answer maniacally for affect. "I am VERY OKAY!"

"I'm gonna call Mumsy if you don't stop." She sounds worried, which has a calming effect on me. I turn the handle and the door slowly falls opens, revealing my disheveled room and appearance.

"What's the matter, Jake? You are so angry...and scary."

"Sorry," I answer. "You're scary too."

With so much make-up, she resembles a grotesque version of a circus clown. The absurdity of our circumstances breaks the tension and we both crack up.

"I'm mad, but not at you," I say. "I didn't mean to scare you."

"It's okay," she says. "Sometimes you just have to let it out, right?"

"Yeah, sometimes you do." I put my arm around her shoulders. "Come, little sister. Let's go eat some pizza and have a puke party."

CHAPTER 3
DARK THOUGHTS

What kind of music does a band called The Blarney Stoners play? I find out when I enter The Heavy Metal Garage. The band sounds like a cross between Nirvana and Clannad. On the stage, Oshi's wailing into a microphone, and Sean is flailing about on his guitar, spraying sweat. The crowd seems to love it, head-banging and bouncing into one another.

I walk towards a giant truck tire with sodas and water on it. I'm in a huge, corrugated metal building owned by a couple of middle-aged guys who work on racing engines. These two frustrated rockers support the local music scene by letting garage bands play in a much bigger garage. Unfortunately, around midnight, they get up on stage, crank the amps and try to sound like Metallica on their expensive guitars. Actually, they sound like dog doo-doo, so everybody clears out.

As I watch the band, and the fans, I'm feeling intensely uneasy. My breaths come shorter than normal, and my stomach roils. The Red Bull I'm drinking probably isn't helping. This is obviously no place for geeks. Studded earlobes, elaborate tattoos and tight pants dominate the scene. I'm beginning to think my white t-shirt and faded blue jeans were a poor fashion choice, especially since there's a blacklight flashing intermittently across the room, lighting me up like a neon sign every time it passes.

What am I doing here?

I slip into a dark corner to hide and focus on Oshi and her newfound career as a singer. As the minutes pass I find myself mesmerized by the quality of her vocals. They have a sweet, raspy, expressive tone which, even though I hate to admit it, blend well with Sean's. His lyrics are poetic too, only adding to my frustration. All and all, this is turning out to be the worst night of my life.

I lurk in my dank surroundings while The Blarney Stoners finish their set. Oshi and Sean give each other a hug and what appears to be a swift, spontaneous kiss. I suddenly feel nauseous. As I head for the door, Oshi jumps off the stage and cuts me off. "Hey, where ya going?" Her face and hair are wet. She looks sexy.

"Out for some air."

"Aww. What did ya think?" She nudges me. We've always been totally honest with one another. When I excitedly showed her my first bike she laughed and told me it was too wimpy for me. When she took the scissors to her bangs following the latest trend, I told her it looked like crap. Now, here in The Garage, I make a conscious effort to give her the truth.

"You were really good."

"You're just saying that."

"No, seriously. You surprised me." I smile at her. There's a moment, a brief second of silence, when we stare into each other's eyes. *We're getting somewhere*, I think, and then,

Sean struts over with his guitar slung over his back. Teeny boppers follow him like sheep, fluffing him up: "Sean, that was so lit." "Sean, I love your music." "Sean, when will it be on SoundCloud?"

He doesn't seem to notice them.

"Yo!" He says to me, putting his hand up for a manly smack. "How'd you like the set?"

I grudgingly smack back. "Seems your groupies like it." I nod toward the herd, then catch Oshi's eye, hoping she got my message: *Sean's a player, Oshi. He's not for you.*

"He's just really hot, and they know it!" Oshi responds enthusiastically, pushing up against Sean. If she lingers there a moment longer, I will implode. Sean smiles down at her, soaking up the adoration. I visualize myself a cartoon character, fumes coming out my ears. Finally, Oshi steps back. "I need some water," she says, fanning her face with her hand.

"I'll grab it," I offer, wanting to please her and escape the awkwardness. I plod over to the big, fat tire and take a few deep breaths. *Pull it together, Jake. This is Oshi. She's not some new girl you're trying to impress. Just be yourself.*

After re-knitting my unraveling nerves, I wind my way back through the crowd. Oshi and Sean are engrossed in conversation, something about a song he wrote for her. I hand Oshi the cold, dewy, water bottle. Reaching through their magnetic energy field is how I imagine going through the Stargate might feel—dense and resistant.

Oshi takes the bottle but remains fixated on Sean. "Brilliant," she says. "I'll work on it. Thanks for giving me this opportunity." Her excitement is palpable, making her even more attractive.

"Yeah, sure," Sean says. "I've got the lyrics in my computer. Why don't you come over Monday after school and we'll go over them."

"Ok," Oshi says.

The nose-studded, dyed-hair girls and boys continue to hover, their heads forming a rainbow of color. Seconds feel like hours as I stand motionless on the outside of Sean and Oshi's bubble. I imagine popping it, Sean disappearing with the mist. Oshi must feel my exclusion because she suddenly looks my way. "You ok, Greenie?"

My cheeks burn. That childhood nickname feels especially embarrassing tonight. I want to melt onto the concrete floor and get washed away with the oil and grease. Sean smirks, letting me know who the cool new boyfriend is, and who's the nerdy childhood friend.

"I should help the guys," Sean trots toward the stage where the Blarney Stoners are packing up.

Oshi nudges me on the arm like she always does. "Well? What's up? You aren't yourself."

I feel unbearably uncomfortable. Sweat dots my brow and I'm starting to feel light-headed again. Oshi puts her hand on my shoulder. I shudder.

"Come on," she says, and walks me over to some chairs on the side of the room. "Spill."

How can I? My throat feels as clogged as the plumbing when Sara forgets to turn on the garbage disposal. Reading my mind, Oshi hands me her water bottle. I take a sip.

"What is going on?" she probes tenderly, making matters worse.

"I…I just think you're making a mistake," I blurt out.

"What? What do you mean?" she asks, really wanting to know.

"Him," I nod toward the stage.

"Sean?" she sounds incredulous. "Why?"

And then I verbally projectile vomit my pent-up jealousy. "He's so fake, Oshi. He's a tool. He doesn't really care about your singing. He just wants to get into your pants!"

Oshi glares at me, then stands up abruptly. "Wow. Thanks for sharing. Like you think I can't take care of myself? Like I can't tell when a guy is hitting on me? Maybe I want him to hit on me." She places her hands on her hips. "What's your problem anyway? I should think you'd be happy for me." She waits for me to respond.

Oh god. I'm lost. I bend over, holding my head in my hands. "Oshi, I…"

Sean bounds up, dangling the keys to the car he got for his sixteenth birthday. "I can drive you home," he says to Oshi.

She swiftly turns toward him. "Great!" She exclaims, then swivels back to me and out of loyalty asks, "You need a ride, Greenie?" Luckily, in the half-light, Oshi can't see how red my face is, and I don't have to look at Sean to know what my answer should be. He's won.

"No thanks," I say. "I'll walk. I need the exercise." Lying is beginning to be a habit.

"I'll tell the guys we're outta here," Sean jogs back to the stage.

Oshi's anger has faded. She seems concerned. "Really, are you okay, Jake?"

The room spins as she says my first name, instead of the embarrassing Greenie. I struggle to collect myself. This clumsiness with Oshi is becoming vexing. I feel like one of Sean's giggly fans. All those school plays Mumsy forced me into pay off as

I muster my best leading man voice, "I think I'm gonna go."

"Are you sure? You don't look so good."

"I'm okay. I need the fresh air. This place stinks." *And I don't just mean The Garage.*

Sean comes toward us. "Ready?" He asks Oshi, not acknowledging me—he's as confident I'm not joining them as he is the Earth only has one moon.

Oshi reaches out to collect me for a hug. She's always been the one to forgive and forget.

"Later, bro." Sean looks over his shoulder at me. I bristle as his hand cradles Oshi's low back. *That should be me.*

I'm jolted by a gravelly voice over the speakers. "Don't go, don't go! The fun's just starting. We are gonna rock…this…place!" An awful screeching noise blasts out into the Heavy Metal Garage, hurting my ears. The owners are up on stage, tuning their guitars, quickly emptying the place.

Kids file out in groups and pairs, but not me; I leave by myself. It's too late for me to be walking the streets. I could call Mumsy, but odds are she can't get away from the hospital. Dad? I never know what to expect with him. He may not even have a car right now. He tends to crash them a lot. At least I don't have to worry about Sara—she's at a slumber party. I text Mumsy to let her know I'm safe.

Fortunately, the Heavy Metal Garage is only about a mile from home. There's nobody on the streets, but I'm so disheartened, I don't care. Some guys in their dad's Tesla Model X recognize me from school and honk as they cruise by, and then it's quiet again. I'm lost in my thoughts when another car slows down, matching my pace.

A deep, male voice asks, "You okay, son?"

Using what may be the little bit of common sense I possess, I continue to walk purposefully, keeping my gaze ahead.

More firmly the man says, "I asked you a question, son."

I turn to look. It's a plain clothes detective in an unmarked black Dodge Charger. He flashes me his badge.

"I'm fine," I answer.

"It's past curfew, ya know."

"Is it?" I say, trying not to sound flippant.

"Yeah. You live nearby?"

"About ten blocks from here," I answer.

"Well, why don't you get in and I'll drive you the rest of the way," he commands, more than asks. As if the night couldn't get any more uncomfortable, I get to ride home in a police car.

"So, how's your night?" he asks.

Not in the mood for chit chat, I answer, "It's been peachy."

"I've had a few of those lately myself." He chuckles.

I point to my house. "It's right up there."

"What's your name, kid?" he asks.

"Jake." He remains quiet. I guess he's expecting more. "Green," I say.

"Mine's Ritchie—Detective Al Ritchie," he says. "Your folks home, Jake?"

"My dad doesn't live here. My mom's at work."

"This late huh? What's she do?"

The Charger pulls into the driveway. I try the car door, but it's locked. Cooperating with him seems my best option. "She's an obstetrician," I tell him. "You never know when those babes are going to arrive at the scene." I hope I sound funny. I don't feel funny. Al Ritchie chuckles.

Yeah, ha ha. Now can I get out of the car?

"So, when's she getting home?" Detective Ritchie asks.

"Soon."

"Hmm," he says. My hand remains on the door handle as he mulls over whether I'm mature enough to stay by myself. I'm tempted to mention that this is our normal operating procedure in the Green household but decide it wouldn't be in my best interest.

The engine suddenly revs, startling me. "Okay, Jake Green," Detective Ritchie says. There's a loud CLICK as the door locks release. "I'll give you a pass this time."

I get out of the cruiser. The detective trains his searchlight on me as I unlock the front door. I give him the thumbs-up and he backs out of the driveway. As I enter the house, my phone beeps. Oshi is texting me.

Oshi: Hope you had a nice walk ;) Home safe?

I'm tempted not to answer her—let her worry.

I text back: Had a wonderful ride in a police car. Shared my life story with a detective.

Oshi: Yeah, right. ha ha. You're funny, Greenie.

My heart sinks. We're back to Greenie.

I text: Yeah, I know. G'nite

Oshi: G'nite

It's two in the morning and I can't sleep. As I lie on my bed, staring at the ceiling, a devious plan forms. When I get to school Monday morning, I'm going to give Sean Haggerty a dose of my particular kind of medicine.

CHAPTER 4
REVENGE OF THE NERD

I t's Monday morning and I've got a one-track mind: find Sean, but more importantly, find his laptop. He practices songs in the music lab, even if he's missing some other class. I guess he's not too worried about *his* GPA.

The sky is overcast and it's beginning to sprinkle. I keep dry under the overhang of the outside corridors as I make my way to the music department. Students pass me carrying instruments—one small kid lugs a tuba. I can barely see his rain-soaked head as he lumbers down the hall.

Outside the music lab, I survey the scene. Like a cat near the bird cage, I lay low, in case some school official is out for a stroll. The last thing I need right now is to be harassed for a hall pass. I'm supposed to be in American History.

Inside the lab are several soundproof practice studios, their front walls glass. Sean's in one of them playing guitar, headphones on, his back to the lab. Entering the classroom, I search for his backpack. I remember it has a San Francisco 49er's logo on it. The other students have headphones on, playing instruments with their eyes closed. It's an eerie sight, so much music being made without a sound. No one pays any attention to me. The music teacher hasn't arrived yet. With cutbacks to the arts, she teaches both music and drama, and usually starts her mornings at rehearsal for whatever play is in production.

I spy Sean's backpack near the front of the room. Luckily, it's open, his laptop easily accessible. Now's my chance to show Sean I'm not the nerdy loser he thinks I am.

All those episodes of *24* I wasted my time on last summer are coming in handy. Like agent Jack Bauer, I stealthily crouch down, and pull out Sean's laptop. The other students seem so focused on their piano concertos or violin solos, I'm a mere blip on the radar screen of their lives.

Sitting low, out of sight, I breathe slowly and place my flash drive into the USB port on Sean's laptop. In less than a minute, the virus that will find and destroy all of Sean's music files, including the song he's written for Oshi, is uploaded. I press the *Enter* key and the diabolical deed is done. I carefully replace Sean's laptop and slip out the door. I can't help donning a satisfied smile as I stroll to the administrative office to explain my tardiness. It's difficult focusing on the attendance secretary as she asks me why I'm late. "Overslept," I say. I'm distracted, imagining Sean's reaction when he opens his laptop. *No one will ever know.*

"Here," the plump secretary with frizzy hair says, as she rips the pink slip from the pad.

"Thanks." As I exit the office, the sun is poking through, piercing the clouds. I feel its warmth—it's either that, or satisfaction, warming my skin. *Today is going to be a good day.*

I'm on a roll, feeling upbeat and cocky. After sixth period, I take my usual route to the computer lab. The morning's drizzly skies have cleared, and I feel confident my secret is secure. As I near the lab though, I sense something awry—uneasiness creeps into my self-assured forcefield. I warily swing open the door to find Vladimir Singh, president of the computer club, waiting for me. Not only is Vlad the smartest guy in the school—senior class Valedictorian no less—but when it comes to computer tech, he's the bomb. Half-Russian and half-Pakistani seems to be a super-awesome genetic combination because girls love him. Everybody loves Vlad. He's eighteen, and has been accepted to MIT, Stanford, Yale and Columbia, all full rides. He's the only geek in the club brighter than me, which is why, when I see him there, I do an about-face.

"Hey, Green," Vlad calls out.

I poke my head back in, eyebrows raised.

"Come here," he says. "Close the door."

The lab is suspiciously empty, and I'm suddenly reminded of Captain Jack Bauer again. He was tortured in every other episode. *Spare me the interrogation techniques, please. I'll talk.*

Vlad points to a chair facing him. I sit, and he begins, "Ten minutes with me, and then ten with the principal."

"Huh?" I try to sound chill, but I'm shaking in my hi-tops.

"Cut the bullshit, Jake. I know what you've been up to."

My mind moves rapidly to decipher what he knows. At the same time, I can't help thinking how badass he is, and how I want to be just like him when I grow up. "Uh, I don't know what you're..." I start.

Vlad cuts me off. "I just happened to pop in here after fifth period. You've been a very busy boy." He walks over to the window. "Truth is, I admire what you're capable of. I don't think your dad can even hack that good." I'm glad from this angle he can't see me smile. Being compared to my father is a compliment I won't soon forget.

A pretty girl with cropped hair, tight jeans, and high-heeled boots parades by. Vlad waves, and I begin to form the opinion that he's ambivalent about my fifteen-year-old acting-out. I relax a little. He swings around and his words come faster. "You can't be doing this here, bro. It's not cool."

It dawns on me that he'd rather run after the girl. I'm just a nuisance, like the fly buzzing the window. "So, here's how we're gonna roll, man," he continues. "I told Principal Becker you were having family problems. Go to his office and tell him how sorry you are and do whatever he wants. Maybe he'll go easy on you."

In my more relaxed state I blurt out, "Yeah, I wonder what that's gonna look like, huh? Especially since I've been using the computer lab for hacking."

"It's gonna look a lot better than the inside of a jail cell," Vlad answers impatiently. *Jail cell? I'm too young for that, aren't I?*

"Don't you get it?" He continues. "What you've been doing here is cybercrime, man, not to mention what you did to Sean Haggerty's computer." *What the…? How does Vlad know about that?* As if reading my thoughts, he answers, "Yeah, real smooth, Jake." He takes the flash drive I used on Sean's laptop out of his pants pocket and holds it up like a prize. "I think you forgot something."

That's it. I'm dead. How could I be so stupid?

"I found it in the computer you always use," he says. "I couldn't help myself, Jake. You know how it is." Unfortunately, I do. Hackers always want to know what other hackers are working on. It's an obsession. Vlad continues, "When Sean came here, upset about his music disappearing, and asking for my help, well...it didn't take a rocket scientist, ya know? I found the code you created to destroy his files. That's dirty, Jake."

Sinking in my chair, I mumble, "He pissed me off."

"You're guilty as hell and this is your only option...or...we *could* call the cops." Vlad puts the flash drive back in his pocket. "I'll just keep this as insurance." He strides quickly to the door. "Go see Becker, he's waiting, and be grateful, man, it could be a lot worse. You're one lucky cyber delinquent."

I pick my sorry butt up and trudge over to the principal's office. His secretary escorts me in, and I take a seat. Principal Becker looks at me across his desk, not with disgust exactly, but with something bordering on pity and fatigue. "Green, what's your deal? Why'd you have to mess with Haggerty's computer?"

I affect my best apology mode. "I don't know, sir. I was angry. I've been having lots of problems at home and, well, I guess I took it all out on Sean." I look him straight in the eye, praying he doesn't call my parents, or the cops. He swivels in his chair and looks out the window. The drizzle has cleared. I follow his gaze towards poufy white clouds in a big blue sky. It reminds me of the Maxfield Parrish painting on our living room wall. Becker and I are both somewhere else for a moment, possibly doing something we really enjoy, instead of sitting here, principal carrying out his duty, student waiting for sentencing.

Becker's voice jerks us both back to reality. "Well, Jake, what you've done is pretty serious, but you've always been a good student, one of the better ones. I know your parents, and

I know how proud they are of you. You and I can work this out between us, don't cha think?"

I'm sure I nod too hard and sound too enthusiastic, "Yes, sir."

"First, you're going to apologize to Sean, in person, and then you're going to put all of his music files back." I start to object, but he stops me with his hand. "Look, you took them out, you can get them back. I don't know how you geeks do this stuff, and I don't care, just get it done. Are we on the same page here?" I nod, and he continues. "Then, you are going to spend the rest of the school year, every day after school, in the tutoring lab...helping kids who aren't as *gifted* as you are." He says "gifted" with a hint of sarcasm.

I don't feel so enthusiastic anymore.

"Finally," he goes on. "You are not allowed in the computer lab until next year and you are kicked out of the club." My face must look glum because Becker continues, "Well, Jake, you obviously don't appreciate what the lab is for. You were using the computers for criminal pursuits. I've talked with Rodrigo, and he confirms that you spend a lot of time in there after school." *And here I thought Rodrigo and I had an understanding.* Principal Becker sighs. "That's all, Green, unless you have something you want to say?" I can sense he really hopes I don't.

"Not really...except..." Principal Becker begins to examine some papers on his desk. *Am I pushing it here?* He looks at me over the top of his glasses as if to say, *You're still here?* I continue, "I don't think people really appreciate how difficult it is to create a virus. If I know how to make them, then I can detect them. I'm hoping someday to parlay that experience into a possible career for myself. Maybe I'll create the ultimate anti-virus software."

Becker looks positively perplexed, but he wearily responds, "Just get out of here and do what I've told you. If you're caught anywhere near that lab, I'll expel you. You got it?" I offer a makeshift salute and he swooshes me out with the back of his hand.

CHAPTER 5
RESTITUTION AND THE COMPIT

Sean has agreed to meet me after school the next day. I'm positioned stiffly by the window of the tutoring lab, waiting for him. It would be false to say I wasn't nervous. Not only have I pissed off the principal but having to atone to Sean makes my innards roil. Suddenly, he appears in the outside corridor with his band mates. I want to avoid a scene in the lab, so I step out of the classroom, over the cement corridor, and onto the grass. My legs jiggle and my palms are wet. I rub them on my pants just as Sean joins me.

"Hey," I say, feeling like a loser, the opposite of what I was going for with Sean.

We stand together in a sunny spot. His mates give me the evil eye and wander over to a nearby picnic table. I imagine they are plotting my revenge. Wiping Sean's music files is probably akin to murder, in their universe.

"Look, um…" I try, but I'm tongue-tied. Sean doesn't let me off the hook either. He's enjoying every second of my suffering. The silence is painful, but he has tenacity, I'll give him that. I search for what to say as Sean takes out a guitar pick and rolls it over his knuckles. I'm mesmerized by how deftly he does it.

So, what's the worst that can happen here? I ask myself. My mind instantly homes in on the answer: *The whole student body will find out what a jerk I've been, and Oshi will hate me.*

Sean breaks the silence, "Come on, Green, get it over with, wouldja? I have to take Oshi over to my place." This last bit rolls off his tongue as easy as warm honey off a hot spoon. It doesn't feel sweet to me though. On the contrary, the old saying, "pouring salt in the wound" comes to mind.

"Okay, Sean." I get straight to it. "I doused your hard drive with a virus which I created specifically to destroy your music files." *There, I said it. Not very apologetically, I'll admit.*

Sean bristles. He puts the pick in his pocket. "Yeah, I kind of figured that out, doofus. It was a low blow." He looks over his shoulder at his mates, then back at me. "And all because of Oshi." He dead-eyes me. *Ouch!* "Question is, *Greenie*, what are you gonna do about it?"

I want to strangle him, but I'll do the next best thing. I'll prolong his pain while I've got the upper hand. "I'll try to restore them—if I can."

He starts toward me, fists clenched at his sides. Startled, I step back.

"*Try?* Jake, that's my life, man!" Sean bellows in my face. He turns away, shaking his head. I get the distinct feeling that my actions have hit him below the belt. *What did he expect? Did he think he could just rock his way into Oshi's world, with no consequences?*

Sean comes toward me again, obviously upset. We are nose-to-nose. With teeth clenched, he says quietly, "You better do more than try. You better get my music back or...," he pauses and looks past me, "...you're going to jail." He finishes with a flourish and shoves me backward. I fall on my butt. Laughter fills the air as the Blarney Stoners watch my humiliation.

From the ground, I give in. "Don't worry. I'll get your music back, but only if you promise me one thing." He towers over me, blocking the sun, waiting for me to continue. "You won't tell Oshi what I did," I say.

Sean shakes his head, "Too late for that, man."

Now nothing seems to matter. Rage boils up inside me like an inferno. I grab Sean's legs and lunge forward. He topples to the ground. Before I realize what I'm doing, I pull back my arm to punch him. Just then, Vlad walks up and grabs my arm. It feels like he's yanking it out of its socket. "YEOWWW!" I yell. Vlad relinquishes. I get off Sean and Vlad offers him a hand-up.

Vlad takes two steps back away from us. "Hey, boys, how's it hanging?" he asks calmly.

"He started it!" I defend myself.

Sean brushes himself off angrily and steps away from both Vlad and I. "It'd be okay if your boy here would get on with his apology and promise me he's gonna get my music back." The band mates are standing now, ready to come to Sean's aide, if need be, but I've come back to my senses. I'm in enough trouble as it is.

"Well, Green?" Vlad asks. "What's it gonna be, restitution, or a nice, warm bunk in juvenile hall?"

Strangely, I think about my mom and sister. Could they get along without me? Would they miss me while I rotted away? Who would watch Sara while Mumsy's at work? I picture a college girl, cigarette hanging on her lips, texting her boyfriend while an ash falls to the carpet, igniting a fire that burns the whole house down.

"I'm sorry, Sean. When can I come over and pick up your laptop?"

Vlad motions for us to come together and shake hands. It's like pulling teeth with no anesthesia, but we manage a fist bump. Vlad comes between us and puts an arm around each shoulder. "There now, that wasn't so hard, was it?" Sean wiggles from under his grasp. Vlad drops his other arm, freeing me. "I'll leave you boys to work out the deets."

As Vlad leaves in the direction of the lab, he puts his index and middle finger up to his eyes, and then points them at me, the universal signal for *I'll be watching you*. Sean's mates, all black hair, black jeans, and tats, have sauntered over and stand behind him, glaring at me.

"I'll text you," Sean says as he walks away with them.

I feel like I'm in a scene from an old Alfred Hitchcock film. Hitchcock was the master of suspense and frequently used a disorienting camera shot called *rack focus*—the camera zooms in on the actor and out on the background simultaneously, creating the woozy effect. I imagine I hear Hitchcock call *Cut!* and the command couldn't feel more appropriate: Jake Green, cut-throat—cut off—and cut out.

I slump against the tutoring lab wall, seriously considering skipping out on my new responsibility, when I see Principal Becker step out of his office nearby. Entering the lab seems my best bet at this point. Standing in the doorway, I survey the row of computer illiterates, otherwise known, in my lingo, as *compits*.

"Hey, who's here for tutoring at three o'clock?" I call out. Some of the kids gaze up at me, vacant expressions, except the rotund freshman with headphones on, devouring a messy chocolate bar. I walk up behind him and say loudly, "Yo, here for tutoring?" The kid jumps, dropping the candy bar and ripping the headphones off.

"Uh, yeah," he answers. "Uh, sorry…I'm…sorry about the…" He points to the chocolate all over his fingers and the front of his shirt.

"Stop saying sorry. Let's just get to it." I pull up a chair. "I'm Jake. What's your name?"

"Paul Schwartz. Everyone calls me Paulie."

"Okay, Paulie Schwartz, do you know how to turn on a computer?"

Paulie laughs jovially. "Ah, come on man, I'm dumb, but not that dumb." He rubs his fingers on his shirt, then pushes the "on" button. While we wait for the screen to load, Paulie asks me how I ended up in the tutoring lab. When I don't reply he asks, "You get in trouble?"

"Something like that," I answer.

"Whadja do? Something cool, like breaking into a vending machine? I've always wanted to do that. Just think about all that candy you could grab."

I laugh despite myself. Paulie Schwartz is turning out to be a likable goof. "Nah, I hacked a school computer is all."

"Wow! Really? So you're a cyber-criminal?" He slams his palm down on the desk. "That is frakkin awesome!"

"Shhhh…keep it down, ok?" I implore him. "It's not that interesting."

"Bet you don't know where that word comes from, do ya?"

"Frakkin?" I ask.

"Yeah."

It's from Battlestar Galactica, of course, but I'll let him have the glory of informing me. "Nope, never heard of it," I tell him.

"Ha! I knew it!" He lowers his voice. "It's what they say on Battlestar Galactica for the 'F' word."

"No!" I exclaim, trying to keep from laughing. He nods very seriously, like he's revealed a top-level CIA secret.

The screen is fully loaded. "Now, show me what you can do, mastermind." I command.

Paulie immediately clicks on a folder that says "Games." I smile to myself. He's obviously trying to get out of homework. My game, *Avenging Maniacs*, is on the school computer because I put it there. It will be fun to watch him play it. "Let's try that one," I offer. Paulie opens *Avenging Maniacs* and moves the curser around, clicking when prompted. He's good at it, making it to the third level on his first go. I'm impressed.

"As much as I like watching you play my game..." I say, "I'm supposed to teach you something here today."

Paulie interrupts, "Your game? What do you mean? You made this?"

"Yeah, it's no big deal," I say. He stares at me, mouth agape.

I continue, "Anyway, like I said, it's obvious you know how to play games, but we should probably do one thing today that's gonna help you in school." *Since that's what the tutoring lab is really for, kid, right?* I'm hyper-aware of my own recent misuse of the lab. "So, what are you having trouble with?" I close the game.

"Ah, man," Paulie is disappointed, but comes back quick. "Um, let's see..." He rubs his chin. "We're using a math program in Algebra that I just don't get. My grade's going down."

"Show me," I say.

Paulie clicks to open "Mind Power Math," a program I tested. This will be a cakewalk.

"Your teacher uses this in class?" I ask.

"Yeah, he's pretty chill."

"Okay, show me," I say.

Paulie and I explore the areas he's having difficulty with, like long equations, division, and variables. He says, "Wow, you're really good at this stuff. Thanks."

"Sure," I answer.

Paulie looks at his Battlestar watch. "Oh, man, I gotta go." He shoves his belongings into his backpack. "Thanks a lot for your help."

"You're welcome, but you need to study if you want to get your grade up."

Two hours have flown by and I realize my new afterschool service wasn't as terrible as I had envisioned. Paulie's messy, and his round belly shakes every time he laughs—which is often, because he finds just about everything funny. But these traits make him likable.

We say our goodbyes and he seems even happier than when I first walked in.

"Hasta mañana, Paulie," I say as he gets up to leave.

"Yeah, *havva potato* to you too," he answers, cracking up.

Maybe tutoring this compit won't be so bad after all.

CHAPTER 6
WHERE'S OSHI?

Sean Haggerty lives in a converted garage, separated by a dense row of trees from his parents' plush, custom-built home. When I arrive, the door is open a crack. I give it a push and drop my backpack. Evening light pours into the dark room, pooling on the floor. I feel uneasy walking into his private space, but I'm following orders from Sean's text: Go to my place. Door is open. Laptop's on the bed. Catch up with you later.

Clothes, textbooks, and musical equipment are scattered around the room. My eyes adjust to the darkness as I search for a light. Suddenly, I'm startled by garbled noises coming from the back of the room. "Blaghhh, blarrrgh, mmmmaaarggghhh, you, you…got chuuuuuuu."

Is this some kind of joke?

I find the light switch and flip it on. The spooky noises are coming from Sean's laptop, which is lying on his unmade bed. I laugh out loud. It's probably because of the virus I planted. Too bad it couldn't have been Sean coming home to this instead of me. Littering the bed are drafts of a flyer for the Blarney Stoners. As I grab the laptop, my foot catches on something and I fall to the bed. Pulling myself up, I realize I've tripped over Oshi's backpack. I feel like someone just slugged me in the gut. She must have been working on the flyer—on Sean's bed.

I stare at her backpack for what seems like a long time, then slink to the floor. What makes Sean so attractive? Is it because he's older, has his own car, fronts a band, and looks like a movie star? Ugh. I'm not enjoying my pity party.

Garbled racket pours from the laptop, making me forget my foul mood for a moment. I brush my hair from my forehead and force myself up. An expensive-looking, angry-color red guitar leans on a stand near the wall. I pick it up and swing it around the room, ready to smash it to bits—but instead, I scream…as loud as I can, regardless of who might hear me. Primordial, gut-wrenching sounds spew forth from deep inside me, as I release the stress of the past couple of days. I yell until I have no energy left. Exhausted and defeated, breathing heavily, I put the guitar gently back in its cradle. I stuff Sean's laptop in my backpack and stumble outside. A gardener leans on his rake and stares at me. I'm too spent to care.

On the route home, I kick at rocks in the gutter. My iPhone says it's 6:30pm. I'm late, as usual, so I pick up my pace. Mumsy is coming out the front door as I jog up. "Jake, you have got to be on time!" she admonishes me. She gets in the driver's seat and the window powers down.

"Sorry," I offer.

"Sara's already had dinner. She's working on a project in her room. It's due tomorrow."

I'm so burnt-out from the events of this awful day, it's hard to care. "No worries. She's in good hands." I hold my palms out to her like an insurance agent.

Mumsy snarls at me and pulls out of the driveway. "You know where to find me." She waves and drives off. I muster a half-ass wave back. I'm happy Sara's occupied for the evening. I need some "Jake" time.

Restoring Sean's music files should be a breeze. In my room, I turn on his laptop and eat the cold grilled cheese sandwich I found in the kitchen. In between bites, I rummage through my favorite bands on Apple Music while I wait for my code to load. A peculiar *ding* catches my attention. A pop-up window displays *GOTCHU!* on the screen. I stare at it for a while, a memory forming. "Gotchu," I say out loud to myself. Where have I heard that before? Oh, yeah! The guttural noises coming from Sean's laptop when I was in his room: "Got...chuuuuu".

"Ha! You're not going to get me," I say to the screen. I run a scan and find out it's a virus—but not mine; the code is different from anything I've ever seen. *Okay, I'll play along.* I search gotchu, and a social-networking site appears. I create an account and play around for a bit. There's a tap on my door.

"Jake?" It's Sara.

I'm so immersed in what I'm doing I've completely forgotten about her. "Go away."

"I just wanted to make sure it was you in there."

"Who else would it be?" I ask.

"You're talking to yourself a lot," she says.

"Aren't you working on a project? Leave me alone. I'm busy!"

"You're such a jerk," she throws something at the door which makes a loud thud.

"Whatever," I say, as I type "Oshi O'Malley" in the search box. If she's a member, I should see her profile page. Instead, I'm surprised by a video. I push the play arrow.

It's night. A group of teenagers cross a street against a red light. They stop in the middle of the intersection and a couple of the guys do some hip hop dance moves. I hear the sound of cars screeching, but I don't see any vehicles. The stoplight changes from red to yellow and back to red again. I'm beginning to think this is a really stupid site. My cursor is hovering over the close button when something catches my eye in the dimly lit background. I can barely make out the figure of an Asian-looking girl with long black hair. The image is fuzzy, but the figure is familiar. I zoom in.

No! It can't be!

I quickly download the video onto my cloud drive so I can see it on my main rig with the 5k, 60-inch monitor. As the video plays, I blow it up and zoom in on the girl in the back. My pulse is racing. I focus on her face, expand, and zoom in. It's very grainy, but it's Oshi, all right, eyes darting around with fear. She seems to be saying something, but it's incomprehensible.

Over the next few hours, I'm a wreck. One minute, I'm thinking this has got to be a joke Sean's playing on me, and Oshi's in on it. The next minute, I'm convinced my virus is responsible for the spooky utterings coming from Sean's laptop and the video on the Gotchu website.

Using my high-performance rig and the latest analysis software, I try to decipher what Oshi is saying. If this is supposed to be a revenge prank, Oshi doesn't look like she's enjoying it. None of the other kids in the video are recognizable to me, and Sean isn't anywhere in sight. Even using the tools and skills at my disposal, I can't make out what Oshi is saying. My hardware and forensic software isn't good enough. I need digital forensics, like the kind in a CIA or FBI crime lab. *Yeah, right. Just where am I gonna find that?*

In between pacing and worrying, I grudgingly clean up Sean's laptop and restore his music files. I'm glad I made a copy of the video because it is no longer retrievable on his hard drive. The Gotchu site has disappeared completely. I'm perplexed. I try to find it on the Internet, but nothing. How is that possible? Unless…the virus I created to erase Sean's music files has something to do with it.

I wrack my brain, going over my code again and again, but I can't find anything to explain this. There's nothing that would manifest a specific video on a specific website and only on a specific computer. I mean, that's crazy! Sure, when viruses attack computers, a lot can go wrong, and I take this into consideration. I hate to admit it, but I'm stumped.

I watch the video at least twenty times as I text Oshi over and over. Normally, she texts right back. I try calling her and leave messages. Hours pass. I'd run over to her house, but it's late. Questions twist in my mind like clothes on a spin cycle. The image of me tripping over her backpack rewinds. Was Oshi there, working on the band flyer, right before I arrived? Did Sean take her to band practice? Why did she leave her backpack? How did Oshi end up in a video on some obscure social networking site I've never heard of? How come I've never heard of Gotchu and why can't I find the site now that I've replaced Sean's files and wiped my viral code? Who are those kids in the video? My brain burns for answers. It's after midnight. Is Oshi still with Sean? This last, unpleasant thought jolts me back to the beginning, and then the questions roll around again in an endless loop. I start to think I might be as unbalanced as my father.

I don't know how late it is when I hear Mumsy's car in the driveway. I dim the lights and turn the music down. Stocking feet make their way down the hall, stopping at my door. I hear a light tapping and Mumsy says quietly, "Jake?"

"Yeah?"

"What are you doing up so late?" Her voice is muffled. "You should be asleep." I let her in. "You look awful, Jake. What's going on?" She lifts my chin and looks into my eyes, as if she's examining one of her patients.

"Nothing. Just couldn't sleep. I'm trying to fix a friend's laptop. It crashed."

"Well, that's very kind of you, but you need your rest like every other teenager on the planet." She points to the lamp. "Now turn that off and get to bed." She moves slowly, one hand on the door handle, the other massaging her low back.

"How was work?" I ask.

Mumsy turns around, and a smile lights her face. "I delivered a beautiful baby girl tonight. Thanks for asking." I realize I've made her happy and that's enough to send needed endorphins to my brain to calm me.

"Night," Mumsy shuts the door behind her. I lie down on the bed, fully clothed. The streetlight shines through my window, illuminating my phone on the nightstand. I stare at it blankly, praying for a notification from Oshi, and wonder how I'll be getting any sleep tonight.

CHAPTER 7
HOLMES AND WATSON. NOT!

When the alarm goes off at six-thirty, I'm dreaming about Oshi and Sean, cruising a cliff road in an expensive convertible. Oshi laughs uproariously, her long scarf blowing in the wind. Suddenly, the scarf wraps around Sean's neck and he's pulled backward, his hands leaving the wheel. The car spins madly out of control, hits the embankment and sails over the cliff. I wake up in a sweat.

Sitting on the bus in a gummy seat, I try to analyze the dream, but give up. I'm too sapped to put effort into mental gyrations, especially today. My emotions are driving me. I know my first stop is going to be Sean Haggerty's locker. I'll swallow my pride because he might know something about Oshi's whereabouts. Exiting the bus, I hear someone call my name. It's Paulie, running in my direction, waving his outstretched arms, papers flying, the straps of his backpack falling off his shoulders.

"Hey, Jake! Jake!" he yells, even as he finally reaches me.

I put my hands on his shoulders. "Dude. Calm down."

"I just wanted to tell you that I did really well on my homework last night, after what you showed me on that program."

He pauses and peers at me. "You look like shit, man."

"Thanks. I feel like shit too."

"What's up?"

"Let's just say I've seen better days. A close friend of mine is..." I hesitate. "Missing."

"Huh? You mean like kidnapped or something? Should we call the police?"

I sigh. "No, not yet."

We stroll together towards the school buildings. "It's just that she and I have a special...uh...bond, and she always, always texts me back, right away."

Paulie puts his hand on my back, "Aw, dude, I'm sorry about that. Is there anything I can do? Ask around for her maybe?"

I think for a moment, "Can I get back to you on that? Right now I need to visit a possible suspect."

"Sounds exciting!" Paulie exclaims. "See you in the lab then?"

I nod. "Yeah, sure."

A few minutes later I'm fidgeting in the hallway near Sean's locker. Maybe Oshi will show up with him and I can go back to my normal state of pouting over their newfound friendship. Even that would be better than this sick feeling in the pit of my stomach.

Sean comes around the corner, an assortment of hangers-on in his wake. He high-fives a couple of guys and pulls a beautiful female admirer in for a squeeze. "See you at lunch," he says, and opens his locker. When he closes it, we're standing face-to-face.

"Jezuzz, Green! What the...?" My *take-him-by-surprise* approach seems effective.

"Didn't mean to startle you," I say wryly.

"I'm late for class," Sean replies. He removes a couple of books, spins his padlock and strides away. I scramble between students to keep up.

"I guess you noticed I took your laptop," I say.

"Of course," he says, then stops and squints narrowly at me. "You didn't mess with my red guitar, did you?"

I bring up the visual of his prized guitar spinning round and round at the end of my arm. "No man, no way," I answer.

"Uh, huh," he says, not convinced. We continue down the hallway to class.

"By the way, I'm curious," I say, trying to act casual. "Did you happen to see Oshi last night?" I keep chill, but what I really want to do is pop him in the jaw. Truth be told, he'd probably flatten me like a pancake. Besides, I don't want to end up back in Principal Becker's office today, or any day, for that matter.

Sean answers my query with, "And how is that any of *your* business?"

So, we're going to play this game, huh? Curbing my anger, I try appealing to his compassionate side, if he's got one. I begin, "Seriously, Sean, I haven't heard from her in like…well… awhile. She's usually in touch, man. A lot." I feel like a cat, rolling over on its back, exposing its belly.

Sean rubs one eye with his fist. "Boo hoo," he says, confirming his place at the head of the douchebag table.

"Oh, that's really helpful," I sneer, no longer compelled to roll over for him.

Sean abruptly turns to face me and steps in close. As he attempts to stare me down, I realize he's not that much taller than me. A fantasy about annihilating him, right here in the hallway, with the whole student body watching, fills my mind.

We remain locked there, for what seems like a long time, until the second bell rings.

"Oshi's a big girl," Sean says. "She can take care of herself. Just get me back my music, Green, then leave me alone."

I reach into my backpack and whip out his laptop. "Here, fully restored." I hand it to him and walk away, his dazed expression giving me a small sense of satisfaction.

Throughout the rest of the day, I ask several friends if they've seen or heard from Oshi. No luck. It's starting to sink in that her disappearance is serious. I don't think I've gone one day in the last ten years without communicating with her. I decide that as soon as school is out, I'm going to head over to her house. Maybe she has the flu and forgot to charge her phone. *Yeah, that's it,* I reassure myself. I'll bring her chicken soup and read to her. It will be like none of this ever happened.

Daydreaming about being alone with Oshi is making me feel better until I remember I'm supposed to be in the lab, tutoring Paulie. Well, tutoring can wait. I've decided that Paulie Schwartz, compit extraordinaire, is coming with me to search for Oshi. It's a matter of life and…well, we won't go there yet.

Principal Becker is standing outside the tutoring lab, talking with a teacher, when I arrive. Great. How am I going to get Paulie out of the lab with Becker guarding the door?

"Green," he nods at me. "How's the tutoring going?"

"Great!"

"Good. I'm glad you find it to your liking." He smiles at me knowingly.

I ease past Principal Becker and find Paulie waiting in his cubicle. A huge smile lifts his chubby red cheeks when he sees me. This could get infectious.

"Hey," I say to Paulie, my eyes trained on Becker.

Paulie follows my gaze. "He puttin the screws to you?"

"Huh? Uh, no...it's just..." Right then, Becker and the teacher shake hands and go their separate ways.

"Come on," I say, snatching Paulie's backpack for him.

"What? Where?" He stumbles behind me.

At the door I hold him back and look in both directions. "I don't have time to tutor you today," I say. "I've got to find out what happened to my friend. Do you want to come along?"

"Awesome! I love solving mysteries, like Holmes and Watson. You're Holmes, of course," he says.

"And how many mysteries have you solved?" I ask.

"About none." He chuckles.

On our way over to Oshi's, we chat about Paulie's favorite subject—Battlestar Galactica. I tell him I'm a Star Wars fan, I never really got into Battlestar, which makes him even more excited, explaining all the reasons why I will like it. I promise to watch Episode One as soon as I can.

At Oshi's doorstep, I ring the bell, but all is quiet. I yell up at her window while Paulie knocks on the door repeatedly. The next-door neighbor, a woman in her mid-sixties, wearing fuzzy bedroom slippers and a floral mu-mu, opens her screen door and calls out, "You gonna huff and puff till you blow the house down?" The screen door bangs shut as she scuttles across her scraggy lawn. "They aren't home," she offers. "They've gone to Japan. Death in the family. Very sudden. I'm watching the house...*and* any crazy teenagers that are trying to break in." With great effort she bends down and attempts to pluck a weed, quickly gives up, and peers at us with her hands on her hips. "Oh, still here?" she asks, raising an eyebrow.

Despite the threatening neighbor lady's demeanor, I feel relieved. This explains everything! Oshi's in Japan. But wait a minute, something doesn't make sense. I ask the woman, "Did they leave last night? I saw Oshi yesterday at school."

"Just the folks, kiddo. Oshi's staying with her aunt."

"Aunt June?" I ask. Maybe she'll think I'm a relative.

"Yeah. That sounds about right," she answers.

"Over on Elm Avenue," I say to Paulie. The woman overhears.

"Yeah, that sounds about right too." She turns to leave, then wheels back around, looking concerned. "I'm not sure I shoulda told you kids that."

"No worries, ma'am. I'm her BFF!" I reassure her. The fluffy-slippered woman stares, confusion crossing her face. "Thanks!" I yell, as we run off in the direction of Elm Ave.

Paulie and I are soon out of breath. We slow our pace. "Oshi's probably sick in bed at her aunt's with no cell reception," Paulie offers, good-naturedly. The thought crosses my mind that there are still such things as landlines, a convenience that Aunt June would probably be accustomed to using, but I let that thought go, as quickly as it comes, because I want Oshi to be there so badly.

Elm is in the older part of town. Victorian-era homes line the avenue. It's been a long time since I've been to Aunt June's, but as soon as I see the lavender house with the tangerine trim, I know we're here. Paulie stares up at the three-story Queen Anne Victorian with its gingerbread trim, peaked roof and the rooster weathervane rotating at its top. "Awesome," he says, impressed.

I rap the antique brass knocker in the middle of the ornately carved oak door. A portly, bespectacled woman greets us. She pulls her glasses down to the end of her nose. "Jake, is that you?" she asks warmly, likely remembering me from 4ᵗʰ of July barbeques and school performances. "Come in. Come in." She gestures for us to cross the threshold.

"And who might this be?" she asks, looking from me to Paulie.

"Paulie," he says, offering his sweaty hand. She shakes the tips of his fingers.

"Nice to meet you," she says.

"You're place is dope," he says.

"Why, thank you," she answers, looking at me, eyebrows raised.

Aunt June ushers us into the comfortably furnished living room. Thick, velvet curtains are pulled back, allowing a warm light in. June teaches eighth-grade English at a nearby middle school, hence the stack of papers covered with red marks on the coffee table.

"Have a seat," she says. "I was just correcting." She flops onto the pillowed couch and puts her feet on the table, motioning for us to sit in the oversized, wing-backed chairs facing her.

"So, if I had to bet, I'd say you're looking for Oshi," she says. I feel myself blushing. Paulie puts his hand in a candy dish on the table and pulls out an orb that looks like it's been there for twenty years. He pops it into his mouth. My cheeks feel hotter.

"Well, boys, I know you didn't come here to have an afternoon chat with a matronly English teacher." She laughs out loud and then adds, "Yes, Oshi's staying here, but I haven't seen her since yesterday. She spent the night with a friend." She turns to adjust some pillows behind her back.

My heart jumps to my throat. It's difficult to speak. I want to ask, *could that friend be a six-foot-tall dude with dark, curly hair?*

But, of course, it wouldn't be appropriate. Instead, I roll my eyes at Paulie. He looks puzzled. I mouth, "I'll explain later."

I don't want to get Oshi into trouble, so I don't mention that I didn't see her at school, or that she may have spent the night at Sean's, even though Sean won't admit it. I have a few more hours before the red flags fly. Aunt June will worry when Oshi doesn't call or show up tonight. I need to find her before that.

"The three of us are working on a project together," I tell June while glaring at Paulie to make sure he doesn't blow it.

"Yeah," he says. "It's about Battlestar Galactica."

I want to muzzle him. "You wish, Paulie," I say, chuckling. "No, really, we're doing a project on California earthquakes and how they are monitored and predicted." I hope I sound convincing enough to an eighth-grade teacher. "We're supposed to visit Berkeley Seismological Laboratory to do some research."

"Sounds interesting," June says. "I'll tell her you stopped by. How's your folks?"

"Good. Really good," I lie to make it easier. Now that I know Oshi hasn't been here, I want to move on with my search.

"Tell them hello for me, would you?" June obviously has no idea my parents have been divorced for two years.

"I will," I say, and rise from my chair. "Well, I guess we better get going. Lots of homework, ya know?" I motion for Paulie to follow me. He starts to put his hand back in the candy jar, but I shake my head no. He withdraws.

"Don't get up," I say to June. "We can find our way out."

"Okay," she says. She picks up a stack of papers and the red pen.

"Nice to see you," I say. "Tell Oshi to call me, okay?"

June nods, busily correcting. "I will."

CHAPTER 8
MALL BRATS

The shopping mall where Oshi's friends hang out is only about a twenty-minute walk from June's. It's nearly four o'clock now, which may be a good time to catch her friends eating salt-covered pretzels and drinking Starbucks coffee. From the main pavilion, the mall stretches in four directions. "Let's head on over to the food court," I say to Paulie.

"Sounds good to me, bro," he answers. "I'm hungry!"

"Are you ever *not* hungry?" I ask.

Paulie doesn't answer, but it doesn't matter because I spy Angie Parker, one of Oshi's good friends, through the Victoria's Secret window. A shapely sales lady is helping her examine lacy bras. I try to get Angie's attention by waving at her. Neither she, nor the sales lady, notice.

"Wait here," I say to Paulie.

I've never had any reason, nor the nerve, to enter Victoria's Secret before. Once inside, I'm painfully reminded why. Ladies' undergarments line the walls and racks. Several women shoppers gawk at me. A dressing room curtain swishes open, and a sales clerk hands a fully-clothed Angie several bras. They both glare at me.

"Jake? What the hell are you doing here?" Angie asks, perturbed.

"Can you come outside with me, please? We need to talk."

Angie is one of the tallest, most attractive girls at school; just her presence is intimidating. With a huff, she plops the bras she was admiring into the sales lady's hands and follows me outside. Paulie is window shopping across the promenade, several large palm trees between us.

"That was a tad awkward," I say. "Sorry about that."

"Ya think so?" Angie responds. She takes out her cell phone and begins typing.

"Are you Tweeting my extreme faux pas in the store?"

"Get over yourself, Jake. I'm getting back to my mom." She holds the phone in her hand. "Now, what earth-shattering thing did you want to talk to me about?"

"When's the last time you saw Oshi?" I ask her.

Her phone dings. "Hang on," she says as she looks at the text and types again. She puts the phone in her purse. "There. Now. You have my full attention."

"Oshi?"

"Oh, yeah. Hmmmm…let me think." She pulls a lip gloss tube from her purse and begins applying it, rubbing the luscious pink onto her pouty lips with her fingers. With great interest my eyes follow her every move. She plops the gloss back into her bag and finds me staring. She rolls her eyes. "Jeez, Jake, you're embarrassing yourself." I'm blushing again. Paulie hears us and saunters over. Angie continues, "Oh, yeah… let's see. Last time I saw Oshi. Probably a couple of days ago," she says. "We went to a film at the Metro." She sounds so sophisticated.

"And you haven't talked to her since? Not even at school today?"

Angie lowers her voice and feigns intimacy. "I wasn't at school today. Don't tell anybody, kay?" She pretend pouts. I'm starting to get the impression that Angie's just jerking me around. Despite this, I *am* under her spell. She has that effect on guys.

"I won't," I assure her, playing along. Angie guffaws, as if I'm a clown who came to the mall expressly for her amusement. Looking back towards Victoria's Secret, she asks if that's all I needed from her. But my thoughts are moving far ahead of our conversation. Paulie giggles as the sales lady waves bras from inside the store.

"I gotta go," Angie says. She looks down her nose at Paulie, who is at least five inches shorter than she is. "Tell Oshi to text me," she says to me, and re-enters the store.

"What's her dealio?" Paulie asks.

I pat Paulie on the back and say, "It doesn't matter, dude. Come on. We have a lot of mall to cover."

At the fountain surrounded by ferns we find three more of Oshi's friends: Zach, Maricel and Julie. Their heads are together watching something on Zach's iPhone. It must be funny because they suddenly crack up as we approach.

"Hey, guys," I say.

"What up, Jakester?" Zach asks in his over-the-top, surfer-dude voice. It blends well with his bleach-blond hair and suntan.

"I'm looking for Oshi. Have you seen her?"

Their eyes are back on the screen; Julie, petite with cropped black hair, on Zach's left, and Maricel, dark-skinned with piercing green eyes, on his right. "Hey, dude," Zach says to me, and then acknowledging Paulie, "…and, little dude," he adds. "Have a peek at this."

We step behind the trio and look over Zach's shoulder. They are watching a video of some guys from Germany taking turns trying to skate in their bare feet on an ice lake. It's hilarious as they tumble, slide, and eventually fall. "Whoa…such pros!" Zach laughs.

Julie cranes her neck to look up at me. "I saw her yesterday in math class," she offers.

"I saw her yesterday too…at lunch," Maricel says in her Spanish accent.

"Me, too," Zach says. "I mean, I usually see her every day at lunch, don't you?"

"We have different lunch periods," I remind him.

"Oh, yeah, right, bruh," Zach bobs his head up and down, acknowledging something he's been aware of for a very long time. *Your gears and wheels need some lube, bruh.* Zach sets the phone on the bench and leans back, putting his hands behind his head. "Hey, come to think of it, I don't think I saw her today. I was kinda wondering where she was, but I figured she was with you, bruh."

"Yeah, me too," Julie says. Maricel nods.

Paulie pipes in. "Well, she wasn't," he says, emphatically. I nudge him. I'm not so eager to let the world know she's missing, especially this group of gossipers.

"How would you know?" I say to Paulie, sounding a little too harsh. I give him the evil eye. Poor Paulie. I know I've hurt his feelings, but it can't be helped.

Zach stands and stretches. "Well, she hasn't showed here yet, my man."

"Thanks," I say. I signal for Paulie to follow. "Later, then."

The girls pick up the phone, scoot together and become engrossed.

Paulie lags as I step lively towards the food court. I realize that it's been a long time since I've eaten, and I'm starved. "Come on, dude," I encourage him. "Let's get a slice."

That perks him up. He's at my side in a flash.

"Wow, I didn't know you could move that fast," I say, and we both laugh. "Sorry I was hard on you back there, but I didn't want them to know Oshi's missing…not yet."

"Why not? Couldn't they help search for her?" he asks.

It's a good deduction on his part, but I don't know how to explain to him my suspected involvement in her disappearance. I say quickly, "Oh, those goof balls? They're too busy stalking the internet. Besides, I wanna make sure she's actually disappeared first. I don't want to look like a fool."

"Ah…I hear ya, bro," Paulie says. We're nearing the food court. "Now, about that slice…" and he's off to the pizza counter. A few minutes later we're sharing a small pepperoni.

"So, what are we gonna do now?" Paulie asks, morsels of pizza showering the table. I try not to pay attention.

"I'm thinking it's back to my place," I answer.

"Frakkin awesome!" Paulie yells, pizza sauce spraying.

My next bite is whacked out of my mouth by a hardy slap on the back. Paulie stops mid-mouthful, staring behind me. "What the…," I say, swiveling around. It's Frank O'Malley, aka Elephant Man, defensive lineman for the Varsity team, also Oshi's cousin. I tend to avoid him because he's bulky, clumsy, and not the brightest gem in the bag. He plucks a chair off the ground and sits on it backwards.

"Where the hell ya been, Jake?" he asks. "Haven't seen you at games for...well...seems like it's been a year."

"Yeah, haha..." It's an awkward moment.

"Howz my cuz?" he asks.

"Great!" I say, a little too earnestly. "I mean, yeah...she's good, man."

Elephant Man grabs my slice and takes a giant bite out of it, then drops it back on the napkin. "Sweet," he says, vying with Paulie for grossest eater in the world.

Just then a herd of linemen stride up to the table. Darkness sets in as they hover, their hugeness blocking out the fluorescent lights. I cover what's left of my slice with my hand. Paulie slides down in his chair.

"Yo, E-man, let's book. We gotta get to practice," one of them says.

The table shakes as Frank uses it for leverage to get up. "Better see ya out there in the bleachers, Jake," he says. Then he walks behind Paulie and lifts him up in his seat. "Didn't your momma ever tell you to sit up, little man?" Paulie is too startled to answer. The linemen belly laugh in unison. They rub Paulie's head and nudge his shoulders, saying things like, "Try out for the team, bruiser," and "Come out for the line, we'll toughen you up." They smack each other on the back, snickering and snorting.

"Later," Elephant Man says to us as the herd wanders off. I unclench my teeth.

"What a bunch of schmucks," Paulie says.

I burst out laughing and feel my shoulders relax. "Let's get outta here." I make sure we exit the mall in the opposite direction from E-man and his bros.

Approximately forty-five minutes later we reach my house. Paulie is thrilled to enter the room with the KEEP OUT sign on the door. He says he feels special. I tell him he is—very few people have the honor of seeing my lair. Fascinated, he walks around checking everything out. "Awesome," he says more than once.

While Paulie peruses my belongings, I bring up the video of the kids at the intersection to show him. "Hey, I know where that is!" Paulie says when he looks at the screen.

"Really? I knew there was a reason to bring you here."

Paulie continues, "Yeah, my dad takes the tablecloths from the restaurant to that dry cleaner on the corner." Paulie's Jewish parents own a restaurant which serves lox and bagels for breakfast, deli sandwiches for lunch and authentic Indian cuisine for dinner. Paulie's dad used to work for the American embassy in New Delhi. Paulie was born in India. The whole family loves Indian food, like paneer and curry. When they moved home to the states, Paulie's parents thought, why not combine the two culinary traditions? It sounded crazy at the time, but now Delhi Deli is one of the most popular places in town.

I quickly print out some still photos and grab the flash drive with the video. "So, where is this dry cleaner?" I ask Paulie.

"I'll show you," he answers. "Come on."

CHAPTER 9
ADVENTURES IN HACKERLAND

We're about to leave the house when a minivan pulls up and Sara gets out, dressed in a pink, sequined dance outfit. She waves to her friends in the carpool as the mother backs out of the driveway. In my haste to find Oshi, I'd completely forgotten about Sara.

"Where are you going?" she asks me, then turns to Paulie. "Who are you?" Paulie blushes crimson.

Irritated, I rotate her toward the house. "Never. Mind. Go inside. Wait for me. I'll be back in an hour." I motion for Paulie to lead the way.

"No way. I'm not staying here by myself." Sara drops her backpack and crosses her arms. Paulie stops. I look to him for support, but he appears concerned. *I don't need this.*

"Fine. Come on, then. There's no time to waste," I say to Sara, marching her over the lawn and onto the sidewalk.

"Where are we going? What's this all about? It's getting late and I've got homework to do. Hey! Listen to me, Jake. What's so important? Does Mumsy know?" She throws her flower-power backpack into the bushes near the house.

57

I stop, twirl her to face me, and take a deep breath. "Sara, I've had an incredibly stressful day, and I really, really need you to shut up, okay? If you're coming, you have to be silent. You have to do what I tell you, okay?" Perhaps Sara senses the urgency in my voice because she actually listens to me. Paulie stands off to the side, shifting from one foot to the other, nervously playing with the zipper on his hoodie. "Lead on, then," I say to him, my arm outstretched.

Upon arriving at the intersection twenty minutes later I confirm that it is the very same one where I saw Oshi on the video. We enter the dry cleaners and approach the ancient Chinese man behind the counter. He's chewing on a toothpick, watching a black-and-white movie on a small, old television.

"Hahahaha," he laughs. "These dummies are so stuuuuupid," he exclaims. He turns the little TV to show us. Three guys are dressed up like clowns, hitting each other and falling over.

"That's The Three Stooges," I say.

Paulie tries to push past me to see. "Who are they?"

"Three brothers from the 1930's who went to Hollywood and got famous: Moe, Larry and Curly. Moe was the bully. He used to beat up the other ones. People thought it was funny."

Paulie nods toward the man behind the counter, "Well, obviously this guy does."

"Really stuuuuupid," the man says. "Hahahahaha."

"Uh, sir, if you have a minute, I would like to show you some photographs," I say.

"Ok, sure," he says. "Show me." I pull out the photos I made from the video, but he can barely take his eyes off the show that is so stupidly funny to him. Finally, he says he doesn't recognize any of the kids. I ask him if he ever sees kids hanging out in the intersection at night. He waves his hand disgustedly and says, "Kids nowadays, who knows? I don't work at night. I don't see any kids."

As we turn to leave, the old man hollers, "Wait!" We do as he says. "A crazy computer man lives upstairs. He's in big trouuuubllllle..." he drags this last word out in a sing-song voice. We lumber back to him, like bears to honey, moving in closer because his voice is a barely audible whisper now. "He's in big trouble with the government," he puts his index finger to his lips and looks up the stairs. "Maybe *he* saw something." Then, louder he adds, "You go up there." The old man points his finger upwards and chuckles, enjoying the possibility of blowing the crazy computer man's cover.

"Thanks," I say, unsure.

Nodding his head very slowly and wearing a thin smile, he keeps poking his finger in the direction of the stairs. I've never been to an apartment above a business before, and I feel uncomfortable knocking on a stranger's door, but it will be dark soon, and I can sense Aunt June beginning to worry.

"I'm pretty sure I know why he's in trouble with the government," I whisper to Paulie, as we near the top of the stairs. "He's probably a cracker."

Paulie looks up at me, eyebrows raised.

"Like a hacker, but one who can break into very secure systems," I explain.

Paulie nods, wide-eyed, as we reach the apartment door. Sara pulls on the back of my shirt. "Why are we here?" she asks me, out of place in her pink spandex on this dingy stairwell.

"Shhhh. Remember what I told you? Full cooperation, please." I rap lightly on the thin door. No one answers. "Hello?"

I say. "Is anybody there?" We hear a toilet flush and water run inside the apartment. I bang on the door. The water stops.

"Go away," a male voice growls from inside. I'm startled. Sweat beads on my brow. I look at Paulie and Sara, feeling increasingly responsible for them.

"Hello, sir, we just want to talk to you for a minute," I plead.

"Go away," the voice says again. "I mean it!"

Sara tugs on my shirt. "Jake, let's go!" Her worry is infectious.

"Yeah, maybe we should, Jake," Paulie says. "The dude sounds pissed."

The sweat begins to roll down my face. I wipe it with my arm, then put one hand on Paulie's shoulder and the other on Sara's. "Just give me a second here."

Loudly, I say through the door, "The man downstairs told us you know a lot about computers. He says you're a genius." I shrug my shoulders at Paulie and Sara. I don't know what the heck I'm doing, but maybe I can appeal to this hacker's vanity, if nothing else.

Behind the door we hear feet shuffling and things being pushed around. Suddenly, the door jerks open a crack, held by the chain. It's dark inside and I smell a putrid odor, a combination of dirty socks and empty cat food tins. I sense the guy is standing there, his hand on the door handle. "I told you, I don't want any," he says and tries to slam the door shut. I boldly stick my foot in the crack.

"Sir, please, I just want to ask you a couple of questions about a video I saw on a website called Gotchu." The door squishes against my foot, hard. "Hey! Ow!" I yell. Sara screeches.

Taking a calculated risk, I shout, "My dad is Justin Green." I figure every geek has heard of my dad.

Silence.

We stand outside the crazy computer guy's door for what seems like minutes, although it's probably only seconds. Paulie taps me on the shoulder and mouths, "Spooky." Sara clenches my shirt. Slowly, the chain is removed. We wait.

"Well, ya coming in or not?" the man says in a gruff voice.

I give the door a gentle push, and it opens into a maze of technology. We can barely navigate through the computer gear. Small colored lights dot the room, and we have to be careful not to trip over the myriad of wires and cords. Sparsely spaced, shabby furniture creates a cheap motel vibe. The man, dressed in dirty, dark sweats, is now sitting at a bank of monitors. He looks to be about mid-thirties. The only light in the apartment surrounds him. Like moths to a flame, we head toward it.

"Hi, I'm Jake." I put out my hand.

"Joe," he says, not offering his. Instead, he pushes back his greasy, dark-brown hair, keeping his eyes on the screen in front of him.

Awkwardly, I put my hand down. Standing directly behind him, I check out his impressive equipment. "Hi, Joe...um, this is my friend, Paulie, and my sister, Sara."

Joe rubs the bridge of his nose, and his glasses bob up and down. He grunts, but his eyes don't leave the screen. Paulie looks at me, confused. A mangy orange cat rubs against my legs. Sara bends down to play with it, but I pull her up. She scowls at me. Suddenly, Joe gets up and peeks out through the dust-encrusted blinds. "What do you kids want, anyway?" he asks.

I was going to show him the photographs to see if he knew any of the kids in the video, but after seeing his set-up, I realize he might be able to help me in another way. "I heard you were really good," I adlib. Hackers are notoriously egotistical about their capabilities. I'm banking that Joe is no different from the rest of us.

He sits back down. "And just where did you hear that?" I pull a flash drive out of my pocket and gently lay it on the desk in front of him.

"My dad, of course," I lie...again. There's a lot at stake here.

"I don't know your dad," Joe says to me, suspicion in his tone.

"Well, he knows of your work." I can't help myself. I really need him.

"Hmpf," he grunts again and picks up the drive. "What's this?"

"I can't hear what the girl in the background is saying. Maybe you can?" Without a word, Joe sticks the flash drive in a USB port. The video plays on his screen.

"Looks like a bunch of dumb kids playing in the street," Joe scoffs.

"Yeah," I chuckle falsely. Sara and Paulie chime in. I shoot them a glance that says, *shut up*, which they do, abruptly. Joe looks at the three of us, shaking his head. He zooms in and out on Oshi's mouth, recalibrating the sound over and over, until my worst fears are realized. Finally, very audibly, we hear Oshi say, "Help me."

Before I have a chance to react, Joe ejects the flash drive and tosses it at me. He stands up and looks out the blinds again. "It's a silly prank," he says. "You need to leave. Now."

My feet are glued to the floor. I don't know where I'm getting my bravado. "No," I say. Sara gawks at me, aghast and tugs on my shirt, forcefully. I push her hand away and continue talking to Joe. "If…if… you don't help me, I will turn you into the Feds."

If there was an Olympic medal for tense moments, this would take the gold. A known criminal myself, I'm hardly the one to be threatening this grown man with arrest by federal agents. In a different set of circumstances, I'd pat myself on the back for my audacity.

Joe sits back down resignedly. He runs his hands through his hair then rubs the bridge of his nose, two habits he seems to be stuck with. "What do you want then, kid?" Joe asks.

"You know something about this video, don't you? Tell me everything you know about the Gotchu website." I try to sound like a professional interrogator, but I'm not sure I'm convincing. Either way, he responds, although I can barely hear him.

"Stone Micro Dynamics."

"Huh?"

He slouches further in his chair and utters, "Buckminster Stone." Joe then lays his head on his arms, like a man who's simply too tired to go on.

"Who?" I strain to hear.

He doesn't lift his head off his arms. I put my ear down near his mouth. "Buckminster Stone," he whispers. And then, a little louder, "That's all I'm gonna say. Now, please, leave… me…alone." The scrawny cat jumps into Joe's lap. He pets it with one hand.

Paulie yanks on my arm, "Come on, Jake." I gaze at Paulie. His eyes implore me, as he jerks his head a couple of times towards the door.

"Yeah, okay," I say. "Thanks, Joe," I say to the broken man, and really mean it.

We stampede down the stairs like a pack of mules and burst out into the street, happy to be out of Joe's dingy digs. The old Chinese man comes out of the dry cleaners and stares at us. "He is a bad man, huh? Wanted by FBI, CIA, you betcha!" I smile at him and shake my head.

I'm not in the mood for a long explanation about hackers with an old man who probably doesn't even know what a smartphone is. I just want to find Oshi. My stomach flips, as I remember her crossing this very intersection in the video, fear in her eyes. It's then that I notice the ominous, black SUV with privacy windows, parked across the street. The engine is running, and I recall Joe peering through the blinds and how nervous he seemed.

"Come on, guys," I say as casually as possible to Paulie and Sara, urging them along. As we stride down the street, I look back to see if the SUV is still there. Sara and Paulie seem oblivious to the potential danger, which is how I want to keep it.

"Wow, that guy was wacko," Paulie says.

Sara nudges Paulie on the shoulder. "You shouldn't say that," she tells him. "You don't know anything about him."

"Hah, yeah," Paulie snorts. "His mom obviously never taught him how to take a bath."

"Well, sometimes brilliant people don't think about things like that," she retorts, and kicks an empty soda can on the sidewalk. I know she's thinking about our dad. "For all you know, he could be inventing a new computer program to save the world." My sister's valor warms my insides.

"Well... I still think he could clean up his act and possibly give his cat a bath, too."

"Cats don't like water." Sara picks up the can and deposits it into a recycle bin.

"A shave then," Paulie says.

"The cat?" Sara looks shocked.

"Of course not the cat," Paulie says.

"Okay, okay, you two…knock it off," I say, looking over my shoulder to see if the SUV is still there. It's parked in the same spot, engine rumbling. I increase my stride. It's Sara's natural instinct to keep up with me, but Paulie lags behind. He's found a coin in the gutter and stops to pick it up. The SUV pulls away from the curb, slowly.

"Come on, Paulie," I insist.

"Check it out! An old silver dollar!" he says, like he's found a hundred-dollar bill.

"Yeah, and it's worth a dollar," I say. Sara and I are walking at a fast clip now. I glance over my shoulder. The SUV is keeping its distance, but definitely moving towards us. I yell to Paulie, "Come on, dude. Seriously. Keep up!" Something in the tone of my voice motivates him, and he jogs over to us. Adrenaline has me on high alert as I try to think of a plan. Do I really want whoever is in that SUV to know where we live?

I notice an old-fashioned diner on the corner. "Come on, let's get some ice cream," I say. This suggestion meets with high approval. I open the door for Sara and Paulie. "Go sit at the counter." I join them, and after a few minutes I begin to relax. Maybe they weren't following us after all. Maybe it was just my imagination. But then, the SUV idles slowly by, and I see the vanity plate on the back of the vehicle: STONE. My heart leaps into my throat, like a kitten lunging for a string. *What do I do now?*

CHAPTER 10
MISSION: IMPOSSIBLE?

I keep watch out the front of the diner while we eat our ice cream. The SUV creeps slowly back in the other direction. I barely taste my double-dutch chocolate; between bites I contemplate ways to give the SUV the slip. I'm betting there's a back entrance. I leave my stool to check it out. Sure enough, the back door leads to an alley.

"Hey guys, finish up those cones," I call out to Sara and Paulie. "We need to get going."

"Why are we going out the back," Paulie asks, chomping the last of his sugar cone. Most of his strawberry ice cream is on his shirt.

"Yeah," Sara says, skipping ahead. "Why?"

"I don't know," I answer, trying to keep it light. "Does there have to be a reason for everything? I just thought it might be fun."

"And it is!" Paulie yells. He tries to skip along with Sara, but instead ends up hopping on one foot, then sliding the other up to meet the first one—hop, slide, hop, slide—he looks like the village idiot. I can't help but laugh hysterically...until...as we reach the cross street, I look to my left and see the black SUV. I act quickly. "Uh, guys...I think I left my phone at the diner," I say, knowing full well my iPhone is tucked securely in my back pocket.

Sara makes a dramatic show, flailing her arms, "Oh, jeez, Jake. Really?"

"Yeah, sorry. We gotta go back. Come on."

Without complaining, Paulie hop-slides his way back, only I'm not in the mood for laughter now. Sara trudges along, dragging her feet, seeming fatigued from the evening's activities. "Wait here," I say, when we reach the diner. I go inside and order a taxi.

Sara and Paulie are surprised and grateful when the taxi picks us up in the back alley. Paulie rode in lots of taxis in India, but it's a first for Sara and me. It's an especially somber experience when we pull up in front of our house and the driver points to the meter, expecting his $18.00 fare. Emptying our pockets, Paulie and I come up with a combined eleven dollars and forty-two cents. Thankfully, the driver lets us off the hook, but not without a reprimand. We exit the taxi, feeling the weight of our inexperienced youth.

As we enter the house, my phone jingles. I look at the incoming number. "Oh no, it's Aunt June." I hang up on the call.

Sara chastises me. "That wasn't nice."

I wave her off. "Go to your room. You have homework, remember?"

"No!" she rebels. My phone rings again.

"Shouldn't you answer that?" Paulie asks.

"I'm trying to avoid it."

"That's just not right," he says.

The three of us hang out in the foyer as the phone continues to ring. "Fine, but I don't know what to tell her." I answer the dreaded phone call. "Hello?"

"Jake? It's June. Have you heard from Oshi?" Her voice sounds distressed.

"Uh, no, I haven't. Isn't she there?" I feel terrible, pretending.

Paulie stares at me, dumbfounded. Sara puts her hands on her hips. I cover the phone with my hand and whisper, "Well, what am I supposed to say?"

June continues, "No, she isn't here, and apparently she wasn't at school today either. I'm surprised you didn't tell me that, Jake."

"I didn't realize…." I start, but she interrupts me.

"I called Sean Haggerty. The last time he saw her was yesterday afternoon at his place. When he left, she was working on a flyer for the band. He said he hasn't seen her since."

A strange combination of relief and fear fills me. *Oshi didn't spend the night at Sean's!* But now my worst fears are confirmed—she's definitely disappeared. I sigh.

"Jake? Do you know something?" June asks me.

"There is one thing…" I hesitate, unsure of how what I'm about to reveal will affect things. "When I went to Sean's yesterday, around six, I saw Oshi's backpack. I just assumed she was with Sean."

My revelation alarms her. "You should have told me that, Jake." Without hesitation she adds, "I'm calling the police."

For a brief moment, I imagine Sean being hand-cuffed and thrown in a police car. Then the vision shifts to me in the back of the car. "I…I wish you wouldn't do that…yet," I beg.

"Why not, Jake? Is there more you're not telling me?"

"No, it's just that…maybe I can find her," I add, in barely a whisper. The mature voice in the back of my head is telling me to cooperate with June, and the police. I mean, who am

I kidding? Am I really qualified to play amateur detective?

"Jake," June says, desperation in her voice. "If you think you know where she is, then please tell me."

I'm stalling, and I know I sound as crazy as a loon, but what am I supposed to say? *From what I can piece together, June, your niece has dropped off the face of the earth, and there's a very real possibility that my computer virus caused it.* Yeah, that would go over really well. The cops would be at my door in an instant. They may already be on their way. I don't want to admit to Aunt June, or myself, the truth—I haven't a clue where Oshi is, or what happened to her. I'm useless.

"I don't know where she is," I say softly.

In a calm voice, June replies, "Well, I must call the authorities, Jake. I'm sick with worry. If you hear from her, you'll call me right away?"

"I promise. Goodbye."

There's a pregnant pause as Sara, Paulie and I process the importance of what just transpired. Then, we all talk at once.

"The police! Jake!" Sara exclaims.

"You're in way over your head, dude," Paulie pipes in.

"I know, but there must be something I can do!" I say. For the first time since Oshi's disappearance I feel like I'm drowning. I taste copper and realize I'm biting my lip.

Sara reaches out and puts a hand on my arm. "We could tell Mumsy," she offers. "She gives good advice."

I turn on her swiftly. "No!" I say, way too sternly. Sara jumps back. "Sorry." I put my hand on her shoulder. "It's just…I don't want Mumsy, or Dad, or any other adult, to know about this. Not yet, Sara. Give me some time to figure things out."

"You're impossible!" she retorts and plops down on the bench against the wall. She scootches over and lets Paulie sit next to her. I can sense they are both emotionally exhausted, and I realize I am, too.

I appeal to them. "Guys, right now it may *seem* impossible for me to find Oshi on my own, but I want to try!"

"Hmm...I don't know, Jake," Paulie says thoughtfully. "Aunt June is calling the cops. Maybe you should let them do their work."

"I think Paulie's right, Jake," Sara adds.

It's quiet for a long time in the foyer as I ponder everything that happened today. Maybe Paulie's right. Maybe I should just give up. But I can't. I contemplate my next move. An idea pops into my head.

"OKAY!" I clap, startling them. They stare at me like two innocent deer caught in the headlights. I say to Paulie, "Can you go to my room and wait for me? I'll be there in a minute. And shouldn't you let your parents know where you are? It's getting late." Paulie gets up, stretches, and without a word, plods down the hallway.

Suddenly, the realization hits me that I'm not being a very responsible caretaker; plus, I should keep a semblance of order for Mumsy's sake. I sit down next to Sara on the bench and assume my best big-brother persona. "It's getting late, you're obviously tired, and you still have homework to do. Mumsy is gonna be really mad at me if you don't get it done. Plus, look at you. You're still in your dance uniform and you need a bath."

"You don't have to talk to me like I'm ten," she complains.

"But you are ten, aren't you?" I gently elbow her. She jabs me back in the ribs.

"Ow!" I feign pain, double over and fall to the floor. Sara giggles.

"I'm eleven-and-a-half, and you know it," she says.

I fold myself into a cross-legged posture. "Yeah, I know it, believe me." Sara kicks me gently, then stands up, and starts down the hall, shoulders slightly slumped.

"Wait," I say. She stops and turns. I call a nearby Chinese restaurant. "Three orders of pot stickers, please," I say into my phone. A huge smile lights up Sara's face. I know it's her favorite. "You can pay the delivery guy out of the cookie jar when he comes," I tell her, and push myself up off the floor.

"You're gonna let me into the cookie jar?" This buoys her spirits.

"Yeah, only this time, because you were so cooperative." I tug on her ponytail.

"Stop!" She screeches, pushing my hand away. "Don't you know you never mess with a girl's hair?" She stamps off towards the kitchen.

"Remember the tip," I call out.

"I know," she yells from the kitchen. "Twenty percent. I can figure it out. I'm not that dumb."

I'm excited to get to my computer. When I enter my room, I find Paulie revolving in my leather office chair. I sit down on a high stool in front of my monitor. "Now, let's see what we can find."

Paulie pulls up next to me and points to my head, "I can feel the wheels turning."

I search *Stone Micro Dynamics*. When it comes up on the screen, I click around the site. CEO: Dr. Buckminster Stone. Location: thirty minutes outside of Palo Alto. There isn't much about what the company does, just some vague B.S. about web development.

"Figures," I say.

"What?" Paulie asks.

"I have a feeling that Stone's company is some kind of a front for...I don't know, something...evil."

Paulie raises his eyebrows. He doesn't say anything, just stares at the screen as if the longer he stares, the more he will understand what I'm thinking.

The doorbell rings. Paulie jumps up and looks out the window. "Food?"

"You gotta go home, don'tcha?" I tease.

"I've got a few minutes."

"Yeah, I thought you might." My legs jitter urgently. I point at the screen. "I've gotta go there."

Paulie walks back over and sits down. "Where?" he asks.

"To Stone's company."

"When?"

"Tomorrow," I say.

"How?"

"Dude. What is this? Twenty questions?"

Sara knocks on the door. "Pot stickers!"

Paulie starts for the door, but I put a hand out to stop him. "We'll be there in a minute," I yell to Sara. Paulie sits down resignedly and revolves.

"We're gonna need a car," I say.

"Wait. What? You're not thinking of cutting school. No way, dude. You'll end up in juvie if they catch you."

"Which is why they won't. I don't see any other way, Paulie." I tap the address of Stone Micro Dynamics in Google Maps on my phone. "If you don't wanna come, it's okay." I haven't told him about the black SUV yet.

Paulie whirls in the chair, the full repercussions of my plan sinking in. "I'm just thinking of you, bro, ya know? You're already in trouble."

I abruptly stop his whirling. "I don't really have a choice. I'm running out of time and Stone is the only lead I have."

Paulie gets up and strolls around the room, stopping here and there to look at a poster or fondle a piece of equipment, probably weighing the risks of his involvement. Cutting school is not something a kid like Paulie does lightly. Finally, he flops backwards on the bed like a snow angel. "Okay," he says, rotating on his side to face me. "Okay." He props his head up with his hand.

"Okay?" I say. "Okay, what?"

"I'm in. I hope you have an amazing plan, dude. Now, can we have those pot stickers?"

CHAPTER 11
GOING NOWHERE FAST

Paulie and I meet fifteen minutes before the first bell in the school parking lot. Uniformed cheerleaders, wearing ridiculously short skirts, practice routines on the grass nearby. It won't be easy convincing Vlad to drive us to Stone Micro Dynamics. I pace nervously as we watch the girls do flips and handstands.

A rusty, old Volkswagen bus pulls into the parking lot. The Blarney Stoners, minus Sean, amble out. I pull Paulie behind a pickup truck. The last thing I need right now is a run-in with a bunch of pretentious rockers with a vendetta. They stroll by, not noticing us. I catch the tail end of their conversation dissecting a new song that hit No. 1 on the charts.

First BSer: It's so retro, man.

Second BSer: Yeah, but it's got a modern beat.

Third BSer: I think it sounds like shit.

First BSer: Yeah, they took an old song, added rap, and called it music.

Second BSer: No originality.

The Blarney Stoner's high-five each other and move beyond my hearing.

"Who are those guys?" Paulie asks me.

"They think they're the next big thing," I say, sarcasm mixed with fake mirth. "Just look at them—they're so full of themselves."

"Hmm," Paulie says, as if he doesn't get it. "They seem alright to me."

Since Paulie doesn't know the complicated story of Sean, Oshi and Jake, it's not worth explaining to him that jealousy is fueling my remarks. "Yeah, whatever," I say.

We wait in the lot as a hundred more students drive in, but still no Vlad. The first bell rings. Will my plans be thwarted because Vlad decided not to come to school today? I start mulling over who else I know with a car.

A shiny, new, royal blue Mustang convertible drives towards us, the deep whoof of loud rap music filling the lot. Paulie points. "That's him, right?"

"Indeed, it is," I answer.

Vlad stops and converses with the cheerleaders, who lean on his car displaying green spandex underneath their white skirts. We wait impatiently for Vlad to pull into a parking space. The loud rap beat stops with the engine. Vlad gets out of the car and notices us. "What're you geeks doing?"

"He called me a geek!" Paulie says excitedly. I elbow him. "OW!" He yells. Heads turn. Vlad grabs his backpack, overflowing with computer paraphernalia, out of the back seat. He strides toward the school.

"Wait!" I say, a bit too vigorously.

Vlad stops. "What?"

"We have a proposition for you."

Vlad begins walking again.

"Wait!" I insist.

Vlad reels around, this time looking very perturbed. "Speak."

"We want you to take us someplace…outside of town," I blurt.

"Forget it," Vlad says, and continues purposefully away from us. I face Paulie, my arms outstretched in the universal plea for help.

Paulie picks up the ball and runs with it. "It's a software company," he yells. Vlad's gait slows. Paulie continues, "There's an exclusive release of a new game today."

I throw my arms up in the air, shake my head and mouth, *What?* Paulie shrugs.

Vlad doubles back and takes a few steps in our direction. "What's it called?"

"Uh, I don't remember, sorry," Paulie says. "But I also heard they're giving away advanced releases of *Hitman 3* and *Outriders*." I nod my head like a ventriloquist's dummy.

Vlad eyes us suspiciously. "Physical copies?"

Paulie and I nod simultaneously. We must look ridiculous.

Vlad shrugs, "Ok, let's go."

We throw our backpacks onto the seats and hop in the car. Vlad revs the engine. I'm a bit shocked that he so readily agreed to take us. He drives slowly out of the parking lot, waving this way and that—comfortable, confident. Personally, I'm as nervous as a guy on a first date. I've never cut school before—another first. There have been a lot of those lately.

From the back seat of the Mustang, Paulie says, "I have to swing by my house for a second. Uh…I forgot to feed the dog."

"What a dweeb," Vlad says, as we roar out of the parking lot. A few minutes later we're at Paulie's. He grabs his backpack and runs into the house. I'm hugely embarrassed. Vlad and I wait, engine rumbling. Across the street, an elderly man in pajamas picks up his paper from the lawn. He stares at us longer than necessary. Vlad smiles and waves. The old man waves back, then traipses across the lawn to his porch. I'm wondering why Paulie needs his backpack to feed the dog, when suddenly, he runs back out with it and jumps in the back seat. Vlad pulls out and Paulie smiles knowingly at me. I'm not sure what any of this is about, but when Vlad looks in the rearview mirror, Paulie is as emotionless as a statue.

The wind clears the cobwebs as we sail down the highway. I don't think I've ever done anything so wicked in my life—cutting school, driving out of town, not telling Mumsy. I picture her sound asleep, comforted that I'm safely hunkered down in first period. I shake my head to dispel these thoughts; I don't want to get distracted by guilt.

I check my phone. Our exit is rapidly approaching. Trying to yell above the wind is futile, so I wave my hand and point at the sign. Vlad exits, and we make our way through a commercial industrial area with a lot of technology companies. We're in *Vlad Territory* now, and I imagine he's happy he decided to come. Life must be boring for him at this juncture—he's achieved all he can at high school, and is ready to be out in the world, stunning people with his badass skills.

The buildings all look the same around here, and then I see the black SUV with the STONE vanity plate, parked at the curb. A small sign next to the sidewalk reads: Stone Micro Dynamics. "There." I signal Vlad to pull over. We get out of the car and stride toward the entrance as if we have important business here. Vlad struts out in front, practically running.

Paulie shoulders his backpack. "Whatcha bringing that for?" I ask him.

"We'll need it. You'll see." He winks.

I shrug, catch up with Vlad and follow him inside. My eyes adjust as we go from the bright sun to the cool interior. Vlad stands there, looking confused. I'm confused as well. From the website, I expected a plush reception area with luxurious couches, indoor plants, and glass-enclosed offices. Instead, we've walked into a large open warehouse, with hundreds of temporary cubicles. I can see the tops of heads. No one greets us. While Vlad and I take in the surroundings, Paulie ducks behind a divider, then quickly pops back out. I look at him as if to say, *What the heck are you doing?* He shows me *Hitman 3*, still in its packaging, which he slips into the front pocket of his hoodie.

I face Paulie and whisper, "Where'd you get that?"

"Restaurant customer. Works at X-box. Loves my parents."

I eye Paulie with new respect.

Long pathways form a checkerboard between the cubicles. I gesture for Paulie and Vlad to follow me. As we pass computer stations, I peer over the shoulders of the busy employees. Still, no one pays any attention to us. I promptly ascertain that they are programmers, creating bogus websites to get personal information or sell products and services. In other words, scammers.

When we reach the end of the row, Vlad turns to Paulie, and says in a hushed tone, "So, where's the free games?" Paulie is ready for him. He pulls out *Hitman 3* and hands it to Vlad who ogles the package. "Excellent," he says. Like me, Vlad's really into games. Age range doesn't matter. He collects them, mostly for research, because he wants to start his own gaming company after college.

"I'll go see if they have *Outriders*," Paulie says, winking at me.

As Vlad reads the package, I stop behind a guy with a goatee and a stud in his ear. "Hi," I say. Startled, he wheels around in his chair.

"Can I help you?" he asks in a tone suggesting, *where'd you come from?*

"Um, yeah, maybe," I answer. "Have you ever heard of a site called Gotchu?"

The goateed guy gapes at me as if I just told him a bomb was in the building. His mouth hangs open and it takes him at least three seconds to recover. Then, suddenly, he swivels back around to his screen.

"Hey, dude, you didn't answer me," I say.

"Never heard of it." Is his muffled response.

"Uh-huh...right." *Your body language sure says otherwise.*

I walk a few cubicles down and stand behind a young woman with dyed green hair and colorful tattoos on her arms. "Hello," I say.

"Yeah?" she asks, not turning around, her fingers dancing on the keyboard.

"I was wondering...have you ever heard of Gotchu?"

Barely detectable, her fingers stop and then resume tapping. "Nope," she answers.

I ask another dozen employees and get the same response. None of these automatons have ever heard of Gotchu, but I can tell they are as spurious as their coding. They know something, or Joe wouldn't have risked directing me here.

Across the room, a tall, graying man in an expensive suit

suddenly appears. He confers with the goateed programmer, who points in my direction. My heart pounds against my chest, but I try to remain calm. Stepping casually over to Vlad, who is now reading the fine print on *Outsiders*, I say, "Time to go."

"Hang on," he says. "Paulie's found the fountain of games."

"Uh, okay..." I try to sound chill as I watch the man in the suit begin to move.

Vlad touches my arm. "Let's find your pal."

"Good idea," I say, pushing Vlad toward the front door, trying not to seem anxious.

"Hey, watch it. I'm going, I'm going," Vlad says, eyes glued to the package he's reading. It's like I'm pushing a blind man out of a mine field. As we near the entrance, Paulie pops out from behind the divider and holds up another game from his stash. Vlad grabs at it.

Paulie senses my nervousness and glances over my shoulder. His eyes go wide. I turn around and look. The man in the expensive suit is walking rapidly toward us. It must be Stone. Unless we are stupid enough to try and make a run for it, we've got nowhere to go.

Vlad begins to walk towards the divider. "I wanna see what..."

Paulie cuts him off. "They went on a break," he says, smooth as silk.

"Oh, bummer," I say quickly. Paulie and I are like star players on the basketball team—handing the ball back and forth. "We should get going anyway. If we hurry, we can make it back for third period." I have no idea if this is true, but it sounds convincing.

"Yeah, you're right," Paulie adds calmly.

"Hey, Vlad, why don't you go get the car started," I open the front door for him.

"But…" Vlad protests. I have mere seconds to keep this from blowing up. The last thing I need right now is Vlad discovering our true mission. Holding his games, he shrugs. "Whatever," he says, and barely has time to get both feet out the door before I close it on him.

The man in the expensive suit approaches, all slick and shine. "Gentlemen," he says. "May I help you?" Paulie and I twist to face him. The programmer with the goatee hangs back. The graying man folds his palms up under his chin like he's about to pray. "I'm Buckminster Stone, the owner here. Are you seeking employment?" A faint, nasty smile raises his lips.

It's the moment of reckoning. If fear had a taste, it would be bitter. I realize it's my breakfast, backing up in my esophagus. Paulie remains too close behind me. "Oh, shit," he whispers. "We're in trouble now." I gently shake him off and stand face to face with Buckminster Stone, the creepazoid who probably kidnapped Oshi. Remembering her pleading for help on the video fuels my courage.

"No, Mr. Stone," I answer him. "We are not, in fact, looking for employment, especially with these scammers you employ here!" I say this so loudly that nearby employees stop working and watch us.

Stone waves, motioning them back to work. He leans in close. "You should be more careful about proclaiming falsities in my place of business. You still haven't told me your purpose for being here. Should I call security?"

"Go ahead, but I know you have something to do with the Gotchu site."

The expression on Stone's face is much like his name. "How interesting," he says, and then adds nonchalantly, "Never heard of it."

"That's not what my friend Joe says!" As soon as the words leave my mouth, I want to reel them back in.

Stone's left eyebrow raises almost imperceptibly. "Joe… Porter? How is my old friend?" he asks, revealing that he knows exactly how I found my way here.

"I don't know the guy's last name," I back-peddle, trying to protect Joe. "But that doesn't sound familiar."

The side of Stone's mouth turns upward, ever so slightly. He waits a long time before speaking again. "Hmmm. Shouldn't you boys be in school? After all, it is the middle of the morning. Perhaps a call to the school, or your parents, would be in order?"

"Save your breath," I say. "But you're not gonna forget me, I can tell you that."

"Oh? Really? And why is that? Are you going to be famous someday?" Stone chuckles.

"Probably, but my dad already is famous."

Stone laughs haughtily. "And who might he be, this famous father of yours?"

"Justin Green."

Stone's mouth drops open as he visibly loses his composure.

I continue, "I'm his son, Jake. I'm a game master, and I could build a bot to wipe-out these scammers' work in two minutes."

Buckminster Stone, owner of Stone Micro Dynamics, is speechless. I start to walk out the front door, change my mind, and step right back up to him. "There's something about you, Mr. Stone, that screams evil, and I'm gonna prove you created

Gotchu," I say softly to his face. Without missing a beat, I pivot and exit through the door. Paulie follows close behind. Slapping me on the back he proclaims, "Jake Green, that took some very big balls!" I let out a huge sigh as we hop into Vlad's mustang and the engine thunders.

CHAPTER 12
HACKER AND STONE

We're quiet on the drive back to school. The wind and the loud music make conversation impossible anyway. Vlad appears oblivious to what really happened. It seems Paulie's ruse of going out there for the free games worked.

Vlad parks the Mustang in the school lot. Some students loiter about, vaping, and drinking cans of Redbull. A security guard marches toward them. Vlad ignores the recalcitrant teenagers; the unruly scene doesn't rank on his radar.

Paulie and I get out and I lean on the car, gathering energy for what's ahead. "

Man, that guy Stone? He was scary," Paulie says.

"I'm not afraid of him," I say.

"But what about you mentioning Joe?" Paulie asks.

"I don't know." We're silent for a moment, and then I add, "I feel terrible about it. I think maybe Joe's hiding from Stone."

"I wouldn't wanna be on Stone's most wanted list, that's for sure," Paulie says. "Do you think we should warn Joe?"

"Maybe, but I think we should find out how they know each other first."

"How do you plan on doing that?" Paulie asks me.

"The internet, of course," I answer as I grab my backpack and hoist it over one shoulder. "Uh…there's just one problem."

"Uh–oh, I don't like the sound of that," Paulie worries.

I continue, "I'm not allowed in the computer lab and my mom's probably home, so…" I wait for Paulie to put the pieces together.

"Soooo…?" he says, waiting for me to finish. Then the light goes on in the attic. "Oh, no, Jake. Not my house."

"Why not? Your parents are at the deli. It's almost lunchtime."

Paulie picks up a rock and throws it. "Oh, what the hell," he says. "I've come this far."

I pull him by his sleeve. "Come on. There's no time to waste."

Paulie lives in a Craftsman-style home in the same neighborhood I live in. His bedroom is a mess. Video game posters line the walls and empty junk food containers litter the floor. Clothes are draped over chairs, hanging out of drawers, and piled high near the closet. From the look of things, I'm guessing Paulie doesn't know how to use a hanger or care to learn. He clears the cluttered desktop with one swipe, and I ensconce myself there.

Googling Joe in every possible way I can think of reveals no results. He probably used his black hat skills to drop off the grid. Entering combinations of Joe Porter with Buckminster Stone isn't bringing up anything either. Frustration sets in.

"Want some ice cream?" Paulie asks. He's already had two chocolate bars, a bag of chips and a Coke.

"Uh, thanks, I'm good."

"Whatevs," he says as he plops down on the bed. Wrappers and empty soda cans bounce around. "Hey, what's so important about this girl anyway?"

"She's a good friend is all."

"Yeah, right, like you'd go this far out of your way for a *good* friend."

"I've known her since we were kids," I say. "I care about her," I add softly.

Paulie jumps up to forage for more food. "Seems to me, it's a bit more than just *caring*," he teases. "If I didn't know any better, I'd think you were in lllovvve." He says this last, drawn out, for effect. I feel my cheeks flush. "Yep, llovvve," he sweeps by me with dramatic flair on his way to get the ice cream.

When Paulie comes back with two bowls of cherry chocolate chip, I'm still at it. "Found anything, yet? We gotta get outta here soon," he says as he starts cleaning up evidence.

"Nope, unfortun—," I stop mid-sentence. "Wait a minute. This could be something." Much to my surprise, in a search which included Stone Micro Dynamics, Joe Porter and the Internet Security Task Force, an article about cases of cybercrime pops up. I click on the link. Toward the bottom, it states: "*Joseph Porter, consultant to Stone Micro Dynamics, is under suspicion for allegedly cracking into government computers on behalf of CEO, Dr. Buckminster Stone. Dr. Stone vehemently denies these allegations and claims that Mr. Porter's services were used minimally for a special project. 'If Mr. Porter used his connections with my company to perform criminal acts, it was entirely without my knowledge,' Dr. Stone said in an interview. 'We have broken off all ties with him.'*"

"Aha!" I slap the desk. "Just as I thought!"

Paulie leans on my shoulder as we gaze at the screen. "So, what do you make of it?"

"What do I make of it? I'll tell you. I think Stone is a

lowlife scumbag!" I jump up, practically knocking Paulie to the ground. "Oh! Sorry, dude." I help him stabilize and do a few jumping jacks to let off steam. "Sounds like he used Joe to crack government computers and then convinced everybody he didn't know anything about it. He probably paid Joe off to keep him quiet, and now the feds are looking for Joe. That's why Joe is holed up in that smelly apartment."

"Wow, you could make a living at this, ya know? You're a darn good sleuth," says Paulie.

I sit back down and search for the Gotchu site again. I've tried at least ten times today, hoping for something about Oshi —anything—but to no avail. All I get are redirections to other web addresses, most of them domain name companies. I say to Paulie, "I've got to find out more about this Gotchu website."

Paulie dances around, punching the air. "Yeah, and…?"

"I need to work my magic."

"I like the sound of that. What are you gonna do?" Paulie asks.

"Hack into Joe's computer," I answer.

Paulie freezes. "Seriously? You're insane," he warns.

"No doubt Joe's gonna have data security up the kazoo. I don't know exactly how I'm gonna break in. We gotta go back over there. You'll distract him while I get past his security."

"Excuse me? I'll do what?" Paulie asks.

"Your skills at diversion have proven quite effective. You'll think of something."

Twenty minutes later we're knocking on Joe's door again. There's no answer. "Joe? I know you're in there. It's me, Jake Green."

"Go away, Jake Green," Joe grumbles.

"I have some new code. I want to run it by you," I tempt.

The chain comes off the door, and we enter. Joe returns to his spot by the monitors, and I follow him as Paulie slinks into the kitchen unnoticed.

Joe runs his hands through his greasy hair and pinches his nose bridge. I'm starting to think that he resembles a mouse… or is it a rat? "So, whatcha got?" he asks.

I take a flash drive out of my pocket and hand it to him. "It's for cracking into anti-viral programs," I say.

"Yeah, right." Joe chides. He inserts the flash drive. "Does it work?"

"In preliminary testing it did, but I haven't actually cracked anything yet," I answer, hoping he'll take the bait. Joe is a top-level cracker, but I think I know the mind of a black-hat. New viral code is irresistible.

Suddenly, from the kitchen, we hear Paulie scream, "Oh, sheeetz! Ow, ow, ow!"

"What the…?" Joe exclaims. "What's that kid doing in there?" He gets up and shuffles in his cheap plastic sandals to the kitchen. I'm praying Paulie can pull this off, because I need at least five minutes to break through Joe's firewalls. I'm good, but he's been doing this a lot longer than I have, and if he can crack high-security government computers, he's going to have superior protection himself.

Luckily, Joe's computer is already on, so I don't have to figure out his password. I try downloading his system files to my flash drive. His first level of security blocks me but I maneuver my way easily through it. Meanwhile, I hear sloshing and banging coming from the kitchen and then hear Joe snarl, "What have you done in here, kid?"

I realize Joe might get suspicious if I'm not concerned about Paulie, so I dash to the kitchen. The sight before me is so comical, I burst out laughing. Paulie has somehow gotten the faucet off the sink and water is spraying everywhere. He slips on the grimy floor and falls on his butt. Joe tries to stop the water with one hand and rescue Paulie with the other.

"I'll grab some towels," I yell. Paulie winks at me from the floor, unhurt.

I hurry back to my download. A second layer of encryption, more complicated than the first, is blocking me. I run two scans to figure out the code. Meanwhile, I rush to the bathroom and grab two scummy-looking towels. At the opening to the kitchen, I stop short and set down the towels. Joe's trying to pull Paulie up.

"Get me the pliers from my toolbox under the desk," Joe orders.

"Sure," I reply.

Back at the computer the encryption has been breached. Will the system files download onto my flash drive now?

"Where are those pliers?" Joe shouts from the kitchen.

"Hang on, I'm looking," I stall.

Popping my head up from under the desk, I realize a third and final layer of security is blocking the download. Would I expect anything less from a world-class black-hat? This is a world-class challenge too, and if it weren't for the clandestine nature of the task, I would be enjoying it. Any opportunity for me to hone my skills is a welcome one. I can't leave Joe hanging in the kitchen though. I begin a scan on the third firewall while I find the pliers in the toolbox.

Treading carefully on the slimy kitchen floor, I slap the

pliers into Joe's hand. Joe lets go of Paulie. "Here, take care of your friend."

Paulie slips to the floor in slow motion. Behind Joe's back, Paulie starts sliding around, doing hip-hop splits and spins. We both lose it, laughing hysterically. Joe wriggles the pliers at us, angry.

Leaving Paulie spinning around while Joe finagles with the faucet, I scurry back to the computer. Firewall three is a tough one. This is Joe Porter code. Every hacker has their own signature style—like a tattoo. He's not going to let anyone in here. With the pressure mounting, I close my eyes and try to think like Joe. I go Zen on it, imagining myself in Joe's mind. I also pray to whatever God, Goddess, Jesus, Buddha, Krishna, Mohammed, and Great Spirit, that may, or may not be out there, to *please, please,* help me through this last firewall.

"All fixed," Paulie warns me from the kitchen.

I'm freaking out. If Joe walks out here, he'll catch me, and he might even kill me—or at least do some serious damage to my person.

"Yep, this is some mess, isn't it?" Paulie is saying much too loudly. "Hey, Joe, do you even own a mop?" He continues, redirecting Joe's attention.

A code springs into my mind. I open my eyes and look up, "Thank you," I say to the great beyond. I quickly enter the code and shazaam! I'm in! I'm downloading the system files just as Joe exits the kitchen doorway. I jump up and intercept him. "Whoa! Hey there, big fella. Look at you. You're all wet."

Joe's dripping water onto the floor. "What a flippin disaster," he says. "Your buddy there is an idiot."

"I know, I know," I say. "Sorry about that. I won't bring

him over again." Paulie and I smile at each other as I guide Joe towards the bathroom. "You need to dry off, man. You got any more towels?"

"There's a couple in the dirty clothes, next to the bed," Joe says as he sits down on the toilet seat. I'm certain that I'm not going anywhere near that pile. I signal Paulie to find Joe a towel. I hustle back to Joe's computer as Paulie finds a towel and throws it at Joe, who begins to rub his head with it. Paulie blocks the doorway.

Download complete! I snatch my flash drive out of the CPU and pocket it. Just as I'm putting Joe's screen back to where it was, he plods over, drying his hair with the moldy-smelling towel. "Whatcha doing there, Jake?"

"Huh?" I move out of the way so Joe can sit down. It suddenly dawns on me that he would need the flash drive to upload the new code I told him about. I need a cover, fast. "Oh, uh…I uploaded my hack code into your hard drive. I thought you might like to play around with it. I gotta go—homework, ya know?"

Joe eyes me suspiciously. "Okay, kid." He sighs. "See ya around."

Paulie's waiting by the door and we jet out. It will only be a minute before Joe realizes I've hacked him, and who knows what might happen then. It's after six. The old Chinese man is locking up as we take the stairs two at a time. "Oh!" he exclaims loudly. "You again. Visiting the bad computer man. You're in trouble now too. Huh, kid?"

"No." I laugh nervously. "I'm still looking for my friends. You haven't seen them, have you?"

He displays some irritation. "No! I told you. I…didn't…

see…any…kids. What? You don't understand me?" As we run from the dry cleaners, the old man continues shouting, "You are in big trouuuuuble!"

Paulie and I jog until we are far away from Joe's and closer to home. The weather's turned cooler with the setting of the sun, and Paulie's clothes are wet. I glance around for the black SUV, but it's nowhere in sight.

"Man, you were frakkin awesome, dude!" I tell him.

Paulie struts around like a rooster, his cock-a-doodle-doo's echoing on the quiet street.

"I couldn't have done it without you," I add. "Thanks."

He sneezes and wipes his nose on the back of his sleeve. "It was fun. Didja get what you needed?"

"Yup, but it wasn't easy. Joe is a cyber genius. Up there with my dad."

"Well, I hope it helps you find Oshi, because I think I'm in a ton of trouble." Paulie sighs.

"Yeah, me too," I say. "I'm sorry about that."

"I'm sure, by now, the school's called my parents, and how am I gonna explain these?" Paulie points down at his wet, dirty clothes. He's probably left Joe's kitchen floor the cleanest it has ever been.

I put my arm around his shoulders. "I don't know, but you have to admit, this will be a day to remember." I imitate him slipping and sliding around Joe's kitchen floor and we laugh some more. It feels good to release the tension. We reach Paulie's house. I feel sorry for him knowing what he's about to face. "I'll make this up to you, buddy," I offer. "I promise."

"No worries, Jake. This has been the best day of my life so far," he says in true Paulie-positive style. "Go home and get some rest. You're gonna need it."

"I will," I reassure him, but I can't truly rest until I know Oshi is safe.

CHAPTER 13
THE POOP HITS THE FAN

As soon as I walk in the door, Mumsy confronts me. "Come over here," she demands. She's holding her phone. "While I was in the shower these calls came in." She presses voicemail:

1ˢᵗ message—"This is Mrs. Simpson from Palo Alto High School. Your son, Jake, was reported absent from all six class periods today, and we received no parental note or phone call excusing him for illness or family emergency. Could you please call the school?"

Next message—Hello. This is Principal Becker at the high school. I noticed Jake didn't show up for his tutoring requirement today. He was reported absent from school without an excuse. Could you please give us a call? Thank you."

Next message—This is Mrs. Schwartz, Paulie's mother. The school called today reporting him absent! We have confronted him, and he admits that he did, in fact, cut school today, with YOUR SON! To make matters worse, he came home wet and cold, and now he has the sniffles. Paulie is on two weeks restriction and he is no longer allowed to be tutored by Jake. We feel that Jake is a bad influence on our son, even though he insists that Jake is his best friend forever…his words."

End of Messages, voicemail croaks.

Silence fills the room. I slump into a chair, exhausted, and rub my temples. "Yeah, it's all true. I'm a very bad boy," I say, sarcasm coating my words.

"I don't know what's gotten into you!" Mumsy says. "I know restriction means nothing to you, but I'm sure it means a lot to that boy. You dragged him out of school today and now he's ill? Worst of all, you ruined a good friendship."

Mumsy, if only you knew. Sure, I'm worried about Paulie, but at the moment, I'm on a deadline to find Oshi. I gaze at the floor, wishing I could tell her what's going on. How I'm afraid the virus I planted in Sean's computer put Oshi in danger. How, even though I can't explain it, I know my viral code and the Gotchu site are somehow connected. How I saw Oshi in the videos the same night I heard the strange noises coming from Sean's laptop. There are too many questions and not enough answers. I'm sure Mumsy would insist I let the authorities handle it. If I tried to explain my involvement in Oshi's disappearance, I would most likely be transported to the nearest facility for the insane, where I would weave baskets for the duration. That's not the worst part. I hate myself for possibly hurting Oshi. I've got to get to the bottom of this, tonight!

"Jake!" Mumsy's sharp tone snaps me back to the present. "Are you listening?"

I nod, turning the flash drive over and over in my pocket.

Mumsy squints disapprovingly at me. "I've called your father to come over and deal with this. I've got two C-sections scheduled tonight. I need to get to the hospital."

Oh, great, just what I need right now—a good, old-fashioned, father-son talk. There's a knock at the door. She points for me to stay put while she answers it. I'd welcome this challenging volley if I weren't feeling like a grape in a wine press.

Looking weary and disheveled, like a seaman returning home after a long voyage, Dad enters the room. Only, instead of sea breeze, I smell his favorite scotch as soon as he draws near. He glares at me and says, firmly, "Jake."

"Still me, yup, I'm still Jake."

Mumsy shakes her head disgustedly and turns to my dad. "I'll let you handle this," she says, and leaves the room.

I don't think either of us knows exactly what this encounter is supposed to look or feel like. We fumble, trying to figure it out, and when we finally speak, it's at the same time.

"Dad," I say. "Son," he says.

The room remains quieter than before. *I don't have time for this.* "Dad," I break in, hoping to rescue us both from any further humiliation. "Why don't you just go home. I'll tell Mumsy you reprimanded me, or whatever."

He's very still. That's the end of it, I think. I start to rise from my chair when he says, "No, Jake. I can't leave. I promised your mother I would speak to you." He sits in the chair opposite me, wringing his hands.

No, please, Dad. I can't do this right now. "Okay, then, go ahead," I say impatiently. He surprises me by leaning over and putting his palms on my knees.

"You are a good boy," he says. "You mean well. You take good care of your sister, and you're intelligent." *Those are a lot of compliments—there has to be a "but" coming.*

I try to be nice. "I'm glad you think so, Dad."

"But," he continues. *And there it is.* "You are too smart for your own good and you don't take care of yourself."

My nerves are frazzled. I feel like I'm about to implode. "You should talk," I mumble. He removes his hands from my knees and flops back in his chair.

"Don't you see, son? It's how I know. I don't want you to turn out like me."

I don't want to take my frustration out on him, but I can feel my anger moving from my solar plexus to my vocal cords. If I don't get to my bedroom soon, where I can research Gotchu, I'm going to say things I'll regret. So, for Oshi's sake, I extinguish my fires of rebellion and muster my compassion and empathy.

"Dad, can we pick this up tomorrow?" I ask him. "I'm working on a particularly time-sensitive project."

The sun is setting, casting a pink hue over the room. Dad slowly draws himself up from the chair and saunters over to the sliding glass door leading to the patio. "But, what about your mother?" he asks. His shoulders are slumped, like somehow, he's failed us again.

I get up and join him. We stand, side by side, taking in the purple and orange shades of the sunset. "Don't worry," I tell him. "It'll be alright. I know how to handle Mom." He stares at me with the saddest eyes I think I've ever seen.

"Dad, I really have to go." I start to leave but he grabs my arm.

"Just remember, Jake," he says. "You are capable of achieving anything you want, if you can just learn to let go of that anger you hold against me. I don't blame you. I know I haven't been the greatest father, but I hope, someday, you can forgive me."

I stare at his hand wrapped around my bicep. He releases his grip. I'm an empty vessel.

I have nothing left to give. I move around him to leave, when Mumsy comes back in. I can feel that my face is flushed and I'm holding back the emotion boiling inside me. She looks from my father to me. Her mom radar knows something's up. I peer at her, tears brimming in my eyes. "Jake?" she implores me, wanting some resolution. She reaches her hand out to touch me.

I shake my head, thinking, *how could either one of you know a single thing about what's going on inside me?* Instead, all I can manage is, "I just need to be alone."

Mumsy stares at me, then turns her head away and I go to my room. Once I'm behind the KEEP OUT sign, I rush to my computer and insert the flash drive. As I wait to examine all the vital information I'm hoping to find, I can hear my parents' voices. Most of the words I can't make out, but I hear Mumsy say, "He's at that age where he needs his father, Justin."

And then, from my dad, "I wouldn't make too much of it, Monica. I remember myself at his age."

It's difficult to concentrate while my parents are discussing me, but I race through all the files I've downloaded from Joe's computer. Most of them are blocked or encoded, so I realize this may take all night. Mumsy's voice rises a notch. "Justin, you've never been able to cope, especially with your children!"

Dad replies, "Don't you think I'm aware of that, Monica? Don't you think I feel awful about it, too? You know I can't help it."

I get up and fling myself onto the bed, covering my ears with a pillow. It's all about them, as usual. Neither of them understands me, what I'm going through. I want to scream, at them, the world, myself. For an instant, I imagine running out there and telling them what's happening with Oshi, but just as quickly, I decide against it. They would call the police or Oshi's parents, and somehow I'd end up in worse trouble. This feels like a bottomless pit of torment, and the only way out is to continue my search.

I leap up and sit in front of the monitor. Files stream past on the screen. Something catches my eye—a folder with the letters STN. Stone? Have I hit the mother lode? Decoding each one, I search for anything that might give me a clue. Most of them are internal memos from Stone Micro Dynamics to Joe about legitimate projects. I feel defeated. The combination of this fruitless search, and my parents' endless quarrel, pummels me like a crescendo at the symphony. Like, at any moment, the cymbals and drums will begin crashing, and I will fall, fall, fall.

But wait—what's this? Deeply embedded in a file is correspondence between Stone and Joe. Stone relays orders to Joe about cracking some government computers. *I have struck gold!* There are no specifics as to where the computers are located, but there are references to military documents and Joe's payment. *Ha! I've got you now, Stone.*

My parents' squabble has become a full-on row. I don't even care what they're saying anymore. I hear the front door slam and then my dad's car start. I hop up and look out the window. For a moment I feel a veil falling around me. I'm drawn away from my frantic search. As I watch my dad drive away, a pang of guilt, and then sorrow, hits me, and then the familiar refrain plays in my head: *Why can't I just have a normal dad—a normal family? Bring out the violins, Jake. I feel a pity party coming on.* Tears stream down my cheeks, but I won't wipe them. I want to feel their burn. I lie back down on the bed and pull my phone from my pocket, hoping for a missed text from Oshi that isn't there.

Out of the corner of my eye I notice a flicker on the monitor. "That's strange," I say out loud, sitting up. Something has triggered the sleeping screen. The reflection of a Gotchu notification box stares at me from my window. "How can that be?" I say to no one. I hurdle through cords and boxes to the monitor. The notification says I have a new video from Oshi. I click the play arrow. The same kids from the intersection are gathered around the edge of a swimming pool. They've got Oshi on the diving board taunting her to jump. It's supposed to be funny, but did I mention the pool is *empty?* Oshi looks like she's about to be eaten by a zombie. As the camera swoops by, she is very prominently mouthing something, like she wants me to be able to read her lips. I zoom in. Her mouth is forming the word *Jake.* The quality of the video is so grainy and distorted, I can't make out the rest.

Just then, Mumsy enters, ignoring the Keep Out sign. "I'm going to the hospital now. We'll talk more about all this later. Promise me that you'll stay home with your sister."

I nod as I download the video to a flash drive. "I promise."

As soon as Mumsy's car pulls out of the driveway, I grab Sara and run over to Paulie's.

CHAPTER 14
JOE GOES BERSERK

We rush across the manicured lawns, swept driveways and black asphalt of our neighborhood. "Where the heck are we going?" Sara asks, her false eyelashes batting at me. I pull her along by her arm, my fingers getting tangled in the mesh of her black shawl. She must have been rehearsing again.

"To get Paulie," I answer. "I need to find Oshi. I can't leave you at home, so what am I supposed to do?"

"No, Jake," she admonishes. "What do you think you're going to do?" She stops in the middle of the street.

I sigh and squat to meet her eyes. I put my hands gently on her shoulders. "You're a pain in the ass, you know that? Come on, and I'll fill you in." She trots along beside me in black boots and fishnet stockings.

"First, I want to get Paulie," I say. She rolls her eyes, knowing Paulie and I are both in serious trouble already. "Then," I continue. "I'm going to take this new video Oshi sent me over to Joe's so he can decipher what she's saying." After a pause, I add, "She looks really scared, Sara."

Sara doesn't say anything for the rest of the trek to Paulie's. Perhaps it's her way of showing support. When we get to

Paulie's, I ask her to hide behind a tree. I walk around the back of the house and knock on his bedroom window, hoping the impending darkness cloaks me from nosy neighbors. The window slides up and Paulie, already in his pajamas, pokes his head out. "Who's there?" he asks through a stuffed-up nose.

"It's me, Jake," I answer in a loud whisper.

Paulie's eyes dart into the darkness. "Jake? Is that you?"

"I just said that." I shake my head. "Come on. Oshi contacted me. I've got another video. We're going back to Joe's."

"Are you on crack?" he asks. "No, way, man. I'm on restriction." He says this last part as though he's proud of it.

"That never stopped a truth-seeking teenager," I tell him.

"You're crazy. Nope. I can't go. You're bad news for me, Jake Green." He sounds like he's mimicking his parents. "Plus, now I've got a cold." He sniffles and starts to close the window.

"I'll make sure you are back before your parents notice you're gone."

Paulie pokes his head out and whisper-yells at me. "What about Joe? He musta found out you messed with his hard drive. He's gonna kill you." Paulie backs away from the window. I wait, confident of his commitment to my goal. After a minute, he's back. "That's exactly why I can't let you go alone," he says. "Hang on a minute." I can't see what he's doing. It seems like an awfully long minute and I'm getting impatient.

Sara comes out from behind the tree. "Well?"

I put my index finger to my mouth to shush her. When I turn back around, the bedroom is dark and Paulie's climbing out the window. "I told my parents I was going to sleep," he says.

"It's 6:30," I say.

Paulie gently pulls the window down from the outside. "They think I'm depressed." He smiles.

The three of us strut down his suburban street, keeping our voices low. A toy poodle pees on a nearby tree, its millennial owner glaring at us as she holds the leash. Paulie tucks his pajama top into a pair of old sweatpants. Sara giggles. He's carrying his tennis shoes.

"Thanks for coming back for me, Jake."

"Are you kidding? You're part of the team. Now, come on!" I step it up, anxious to find out what Oshi is trying to tell me. Sara follows closely, but Paulie, as usual, trails way behind as he hops along, trying to put one shoe on, and then the other. We stop and wait for him, then march down the street side-by-side, like the tinman, lion, and scarecrow, on our way to see the wizard.

It's almost dark by the time we reach Joe's. I take several deep breaths preparing myself, as we climb the stairs.

"You got some big cajones coming here, Jake," Joe says through the door. Paulie smirks and nods his head as if to say, *I told you so.*

"Please, let me in. I can explain everything," I plead.

"You kids are nothing but trouble," Joe adds. "I trusted you, Jake, and you hacked me."

I glance down the stairs. A man and woman are exiting the cleaners. I put my mouth closer to the door and lower my voice. "I'm sorry. You're right. If it's any consolation, it was extremely difficult. Your security is the best!"

The chain falls on the inside of the door. Sara, Paulie and I stare at each other. For all we know, Joe Porter could be holding a baseball bat. I put my hand on the knob, turn it slowly, and peek inside.

My first thought is that perhaps Joe doesn't get much human contact. Maybe we're filling some hole in his life. Whatever it is, he's letting us back in to his skuzzy, slimy, smelly, stained apartment. Joe drags his grouchy self to his computer area; the place where I fantasize he battles the forces of evil, like corrupt governments and greedy, mega-corporations. I find I'm beginning to like Joe. He pinches his nose again and I definitely see a mouse, not a rat.

Paulie has decided to stay close to the door in case Joe loses his temper. Sara is nosing around the apartment. The orange cat finds its way to her and this time I don't chastise her when she reaches down to pet it.

"How'd ya get past level 3?" Joe calmly asks me, sitting back down at his desk.

"It was tough," I say. "I had to use all the skills my father taught me, and even then, I wasn't sure I was gonna be able to crack it."

"You coulda just asked me, ya know."

"What? The code for your firewalls?"

"No, about the Gotchu site," he says. *I thought I did.*

I want to hug him. Instead, I put my hand on his shoulder. My flash drive dangles from my fingers. "We'll get to that," I say. "Can you decipher this for me first?"

"What is it?" he asks.

"Another video of my girlfr…of Oshi. I can't make out what she's saying, and I'm really worried about her."

Joe gets up and peeks through the blinds. I peek out, too. No black SUV. Joe looks at me. Words aren't necessary. There is camaraderie between us, an understanding. He goes back to his desk and puts the flash drive in the USB port.

I'm impressed watching Joe finesse his sound and digital equipment. Who knows how he managed to get his hands on this kind of hardware. I'll have to ask him about it someday, when time isn't of the essence, and we can just hang out, two hackers, sharing strategies and stories.

Sara and Paulie wander over to watch Joe manipulate the image of Oshi, syncing the sound to her mouth movements. It takes some time, but finally we clearly hear her say, "Jake, I'm stuck in here. Please, help!"

"What does she mean she's stuck in there?" I ask Joe. "Stuck in where?"

"Sounds like she's stuck in the computer," Paulie laughs. "Ha-ha…stuck in a website! Like that could ever happen." He convulses until he notices no one else is. Sara and I glare at him.

Joe isn't paying attention to any of this. He looks troubled. Suddenly, he gets up and careens around the room, picking up papers, looking at them and then flinging them, one at a time, over his shoulders. His cheap dining table is covered with files. We watch in amazement as he shoves them all to the floor, then squats and rapidly goes through them. "I know it's here somewhere!" he shouts. He hurls the files and documents about. He has gone berserk!

"Joe, what are you searching for?" I ask him.

"Paranormal experimentation. Where is that report? Computer code, meshing with the human energy field," he babbles.

"Hey, slow down, man. I want to understand what you're saying." I follow him around the room, tripping over one of his cords and nearly taking out a piece of equipment. Joe's cat hisses.

"Military...early 90's...top-secret..." he continues, working himself into a frenzy. "Probably just fantasies, like Big Foot or the Loch Ness Monster." Joe stops, runs his hand through his hair, then darts around the room again, yanking open closets and drawers. Sara and Paulie hold onto each other by the door, frightened. I close my eyes and take deep breaths as I try to connect the dots of Joe's rampage. I need to get him to focus.

"Hey, Joe, none of this is making any sense. Come and sit down here." I point to a lumpy chair near the door. "Explain to me what you're babbling about."

Joe doesn't sit but continues to rifle through piles stacked around the small apartment. Suddenly, he stops and gazes, glassy-eyed, as though he's looking at an invisible screen. Then, he says slowly, "A professor...at Stanford...Dr. Lavinski. Yeah...I remember now...he was involved with the program." And then, just as suddenly, he races, sliding in his slippers, to a five-foot-tall stack of files in the corner. He drops them one by one to the floor.

"Where is that damn file!" Joe yells. Finally, he holds up a yellowed folder. "Aha!" He steps pointedly over to me and shakes it in my face. "I knew it was here." Dropping into the lumpy chair, Joe opens the file folder and extracts an old, weathered document. "I knew it was here," he says again, less agitated. He slowly extends the document toward me. I accept it from his tired hand. "Be careful," he says, and then falls asleep exhausted in the chair. I put a dirty afghan over him, and we leave the apartment.

CHAPTER 15
IN OVER OUR HEADS

At the bottom of the stairs, I suddenly stop short, causing Paulie and Sara to crash into me. They both screech.

"Shhhh," I admonish them. Through the glass door I see the black SUV pull up and park across the street. A huge man with gargantuan arm muscles gets out of the back seat and holds the door open. Buckminster Stone steps out onto the pavement, smoothes his tailored suit and begins to cross the street toward Joe's. I carefully tuck the document into the back of my pants and cover it with my shirt. We are prisoners in a tiny lobby. The fluorescent light on the ceiling flashes on and off, needing new tubes. The only other light comes from the streetlamps outside. The darkness in the stairwell provides some camouflage. My mind searches for a way out. I hop off the first step and try the door to the cleaners. It's locked. All that stands between us and Stone is the glass door leading to the street.

"Come on," I say, pulling Sara back up the stairs with me.

"What's going on, Jake?" Sara asks, fear in her voice.

"Don't worry," I assure her. "Just do as I say."

Fueled by adrenaline, the three of us race up the stairs and quietly slip back into Joe's apartment. He's still passed out in the chair. I put my finger to my mouth, signaling them to be quiet. "Hide," I whisper. Comical in every circumstance, Paulie strides gingerly over to the bathroom, and slips in behind the shower curtain. Sara, using her bountiful wits, tiptoes softly to the kitchen, where she fits easily inside a kitchen cabinet.

The front door flies open just as I squeeze into the small closet near the chair where Joe is passed out. Two of Stone's bodyguards enter. The big goons must have thought the door was locked, because they stumble over each other from excessive force. Stone crosses the threshold behind them. "Well, that was much easier than I expected," he says. The closet door doesn't shut properly, leaving a crack to see through. In this cramped space, my breathing sounds as loud as Darth Vader's. I hope I'm the only one who can hear it.

Joe rouses and gazes around bewildered, then realizes who is standing in front of him. "Hello, Joe," Stone says, standing uncomfortably close. Stone is tall, at least six foot two, and I must admit he looks menacing with his gelled hair and shiny suit. Signaling his guys to dismantle the computer area, he orders, "Bring it all."

Joe sits upright. "What the...? Hey, stop that," he yells at Stone's men.

"Such a pity, Joe," Stone says, crossing one hand over the other at the bottom of his suit jacket. "I didn't think we would see each other again. At least, that was the agreement."

"I haven't.... I didn't...," Joe stammers.

Stone unfastens his bottom button. He glances around for a place to sit but reconsiders and remains standing. "Please don't debase yourself with these protestations. We both know you've breeched your contract."

"It's those damn kids. They're on to something," Joe says.

I want to gasp, but I focus on keeping my breathing as quiet as possible. *Thanks a lot Joe. Save your own butt.* I'd probably do the same thing under the circumstances.

I wonder how Sara and Paulie are holding up, and pray they remain still. Suddenly, Stone turns and peers in the direction of the closet. I hold my breath, as if he can see the shallow movement of my lungs. "I'll deal with those nosy kids, later," he says, practically spitting the words. My heart pounds so loudly in my ears I think he must hear it too, but, instead, he wheels back towards Joe. I slowly release my breath. "For right now," he continues, "I think you're safer in my custody, Joe."

Stone's thugs pile computer equipment by the front door, taking little care with it. Joe's face sags. I feel his pain; all that sensitive equipment being tussled about by ruffians. It's enough to make any geek lose their lunch.

"I think we're finished here, Mr. Stone," one of them says.

"Not quite," Stone answers and gestures for them to take Joe. I want to protest, but I realize any attempt to save Joe would endanger Paulie and Sara. The two hulking men approach Joe, who struggles feebly. One ties his hands behind his back as the other throws a black bag over his head.

"Hey, what're you doing?" Joe cries, but no one pays attention. They lead him past the closet and push him out the door of the apartment.

Stone pulls a wireless headset out of his pocket and sticks it in his ear. He pushes a button on it and says, "Come get this criminal's stuff." I hear Joe's protestations as he's ushered down the stairs. My heart sinks, knowing there's nothing I can do for him. I pray this nightmare will be over soon. Unfortunately, in less than a minute, a third man, larger than the first two, with a jagged scar across his cheek, enters the apartment. He hoists a massive amount of hardware and hauls it out the door. One of the first two thugs reappears and removes more equipment. Stone stays behind, browsing through the papers Joe has strewn about. He picks one up and examines it. "Hmmpf," he exclaims, then, narrowing his eyes towards the slit in the closet door, he lets it float to the floor. I think about the document Joe gave me, tucked safely in the back of my pants.

I hear loud, bounding footsteps on the stairs. Stone's three goliaths re-enter the room. They stand at the ready, like giant Labrador retrievers waiting for a ball to fetch. Stone orders them. "You two…" He points. "Take the rest of that equipment. And you…" He points to the beast with the scar. "Take care of this place." I swear Stone is looking directly at me. With venom, he adds, "Torch it if you have to." With this last statement, Stone vanishes out the door.

Inside the closet, I gulp. What must Paulie and Sara be thinking? I will them to remain calm. After Stone leaves, the scarred man slowly tours the apartment, weighing his task. He looks out the blinds and then sits down at the empty computer desk, flicking a lighter between his thumb and index finger.

And then, my cell phone rings! *Why didn't I turn it off? No time to think.*

I quickly silence my phone, but it's too late—Scarman's eyes dart in the direction of the sound. He's stomping toward the closet. I'm dead. I feel around behind me for something—anything—that might save my life. *A broom? It'll have to do.* I grasp the handle. When Scarman yanks opens the closet door, I surprise him with a thrust to the groin area. He doubles over and then suddenly, Paulie appears with the shower curtain which he throws over Scarman's head, disorienting him further.

"SARA!" I shout. "Get out here!"

Sara is already on her way out of the kitchen. She's hoisting a cast iron frying pan. Scarman is trying to regain his balance when Sara whops him on the head with the pan. It doesn't knock him out, like you see in the movies, because, well, that stuff only happens in the movies—and, besides, Sara is eleven and doesn't have that kind of strength. However, the conk with the pan tips him off balance enough to send him sprawling onto the floor. It's the *one-two-three* attack that throws him off guard to give us enough time to fly down the stairs. I'm worried about the SUV, but anything's better than being turned into burnt toast.

As soon as we're out the glass door, I skid to a stop and look in both directions to make sure Stone is gone. No SUV in sight. He's probably thinking this building is up in flames by now, with us in it. "Come on!" I yell, and we tear down the street. Our victim comes barreling out the door and sees us, his massive frame exploding into a full run. He'll be on us faster than a frog's tongue on a bug. Suddenly, headlights are visible, coming in our direction. I pray they reach us before our pursuer does. I wave my arms frantically. The car stops in the middle of the road. So does Scarman. The driver side window powers down.

"You kids okay?" a normal-looking guy, forty-something,

asks. He's driving a used BMW, wearing a business suit, his tie undone, probably on his way home from work. He doesn't look like the serial killer type, although, I can't say as I've ever met a serial killer, so how would I know? Most of them probably look pretty normal, like this guy. I immediately shake off this thought pattern. We're in a huge bind here and I've got to break one of the oldest rules in the book—never accept a ride from a stranger.

I lean on the guy's door and look over my shoulder. Scarman is hovering, in the middle of the street, waiting, probably trying to assess the situation and decide what to do. I never thought I would be in the position of having to decide between a ride with a potential murderer, or being hunted down by a scar-faced arsonist.

I gather my wits, "Thanks for stopping, sir. That creepy guy back there has been following us. Mind if we catch a ride?"

"Hop in," he says.

Sara looks worried, but I open the back door and push her in. Paulie swoops in beside her, practically knocking her over. I run around to the passenger front. The driver puts the car into gear, and we move forward.

"Uh, would you mind not driving past that guy?" I ask.

"No problemo," the driver responds. "Do you want me to call the police?"

"Nah, that's okay. There's a lot of crazy people out there these days," I chuckle nervously. *I mean, our driver could be one of them.*

"Yuh, I hear ya," the driver says, as he makes a U-turn, holding our precious lives in his hands. As the car makes the wide turn and drives away, I watch Scarman get smaller and smaller in the side mirror. I see him take out his cell phone—calling Stone, no doubt. I reach around and touch the document, feeling it safe against my skin, and breathe a deep satisfying breath of fresh air.

CHAPTER 16
INTERROGATION

The driver of the BMW turns out to be a nice guy who likes to talk. By the time we reach our neighborhood, we know his name is Jim and he was the quarterback at Palo Alto High eons ago. He has three kids, ages ten, thirteen and sixteen, who drive him crazy, and his wife has an eating disorder. Fortunately, he didn't go into the details. He seems more interested in baring his soul to three strange kids, than showing concern for the circumstances we find ourselves in. When he drops us off near Paulie's, we express our thanks. I'm especially grateful he wasn't a serial killer. We wave goodbye and head over to Paulie's where I boost him safely back through his bedroom window without incident.

Sara and I jog the three blocks home. I'm anxious to study the document Joe rooted out from the chaos he calls home. A moment of grief stabs my heart, as I remember Joe being escorted out of the apartment with a black bag over his head. The next thought is too painful to contemplate, so I let it go, at least for the present.

Thankfully, I don't have to coerce Sara into leaving me alone tonight. Spent and weary, she willingly trudges off to take her bath.

"I'll order a pizza if you want," I call after her.

"I'm not hungry," she says.

"You okay?" I ask, as I watch her totter, like a tired puppy.

She stops and regards me. "Yeah, I just want to wash away the fear. Are you okay?"

"I will be, once I've found Oshi."

Sara nods as if that's all the energy she has left and continues down the hall. I know I'm asking a lot of her, and she's turning out to be an adept accomplice. Recalling how she blasted that barbarian with the frying pan makes me smile. I remove the document from the back of my pants and enter my bedroom. I'm just about to look at it when the doorbell rings.

"Who's that?" Sara calls from the bathroom. Her voice sounds tense.

"I guess I won't know until I answer it, will I?" I call back. "Don't worry." I barely convince myself. Has Scarface some-how managed to find us? I hide the document and shut my bedroom door.

Detective Al Ritchie stares at me through the peep hole in the front door. Expecting to see our attacker, instead I'm relieved. As I open the door the police walkie-talkie booms, "Code 6, 2042 Lyon St., suspect may be armed and dangerous." Detective Ritchie calmly turns down his walkie.

"Do you need to…uh… respond to that?" I ask.

"Not my watch," he answers in a curt professional tone.

"Oh."

Am I supposed to invite him in? I'm not sure of the protocol when a police detective knocks on your door. Another first for me, although I'm starting to think it won't be my last.

"Jake? Isn't it?" He asks, peering over my head. "I'm here to ask you some questions about a missing girl. Mind if I come in?" *Is there an option here?*

"Uh...sure." I say, opening the door wider.

Detective Ritchie enters the foyer. The last time I saw him we were sitting in a dark cruiser. Now, in the light, I notice that he looks to be in his early forties, physically fit and not bad looking. The police radio in his squad car continues to broadcast crimes taking place at this very moment. Neighbors watch from their yards or porches. I close the door to their intrusive curiousness. I'm apprehensive about being interrogated by a cop, but how long could I expect Aunt June to wait? My efforts at finding Oshi have thus far been dismal. I invite him to follow me into the living room. He takes the couch. I take the chair opposite. It's quiet for a minute, until I break the ice.

"Different vehicle tonight."

Al shifts his weight on the couch. "Yeah, different duty. We all take different shifts, ya know, pitch in. Especially when there's a kid missing." He catches my eyes and stares.

"So, this is about Oshi, isn't it?" I ask, heading him off at the pass.

"I understand from her aunt that you know her quite well," he responds, unmoved.

"Yeah, her aunt called me last night asking if I'd seen her. I thought she was staying there while her parents are in Japan." I try to sound convincing.

His tone becomes stern, letting me know he means business.

"Her parents *were* in Japan, but I understand they're on a plane home as we speak. Their fifteen-year-old daughter hasn't been seen in over forty-eight hours and I heard *you* may know something about it." He looks me dead in the eye again. I'm like a tiger in a cage—nowhere to run, nowhere to hide. I stand up.

"Where do you think you're going?" the officer asks.

"Out to search for her, of course!"

Detective Ritchie softens, just a bit. "That's not a good idea, Jake. Please, sit down." I obey, flopping back down into the chair. He takes a notepad and pen out of his shirt pocket.

"When was the last time you saw Oshi?"

"Yesterday." *Or was it the day before yesterday?* "It was a couple of days ago, I guess, at school." *The truth is, I've lost track. It's all a blur.*

"Her aunt…" he stops to look at his notes, "…June…said something about a backpack?" He reads from his notes: "Jake Green said he saw Oshi's backpack at Sean Haggerty's the day before yesterday."

"Yes, that's true. I went over there to pick up Sean's laptop and while I was there, I saw Oshi's backpack. I didn't see her though." My mind is reeling, trying to cover my tracks.

"Weren't you wondering where she was?" he asks, with seemingly genuine concern.

"Nah. I figured she was with Sean," I say, casually, as if I didn't care a single iota about whether Oshi was with Sean or not. I should be nominated for this performance.

Ritchie checks his notes again. "Haggerty. Yes. We interviewed him." He reads in a monotone voice: "I left Oshi at my house working on a band flyer. When I got back home, she was gone. I didn't think much about it."

"Ah," I say, thoughtfully. I know all of this, of course, but I try to sound like I'm hearing it for the first time.

"So, you have no idea where Oshi might have gone?"

"I went to her house yesterday and the neighbor said she was staying with her aunt. So, I visited her, and she said Oshi had spent the night with a friend."

"Where do you think she spent the night?" he asks.

"I haven't a clue." For once, I'm telling the truth.

"Are you friends with Sean Haggerty?" he asks.

I laugh out loud.

"I guess that answers that," he says.

"What about other friends? Can you give me some names of people I can contact?" For the next several minutes he writes down some names I give him. "Anybody else?" he asks.

"That's all I can think of." *I'm ready to be done with this, Al. I've got important sleuthing to do myself.*

"Your mom delivering babies tonight?" he asks.

"Yeah. You never know when they're going to arrive at the scene." I force a fake smile and he smiles back, remembering I said this to him that night in the cruiser.

Detective Ritchie rises from the comfortable couch. Maybe he enjoyed having a fifteen-minute reprieve from responding to dispatches. "Don't do anything rash about your friend," he says. *I wouldn't think of it, sir!* He traverses the short space between the living room and the front door in a few businesslike steps. I follow. "If you hear anything, give the department a call." He hands me a card with his number. I hold the card tightly. It's a double-edged sword seeing him go; even though I'm nervous about withholding information, I feel safer with him here.

"Good night," he says in an official tone, then turns up his walkie. I hear it announce, "Code 10—armed robbery, 2260 Walker Rd."

"My watch," he says and winks. He dashes for his car and dives in the driver's seat. There's a *whoop whoop* sound and the red lights go on as he makes a U-turn and careens toward the crime scene. I close the front door and lean against it, letting out a sigh—and a day's worth of pent-up tension with it.

As I walk back to my room to peruse the document, Sara calls from the tub, "Who was that?"

"Just a life insurance salesman," I answer. "I didn't buy any." *Although maybe I should.*

CHAPTER 17

SCARY SCIFI STUFF

I smooth the document out on my desk. Its age shows, in yellowed paper and chewed edges. The binding is cracked, barely holding together the back and front cover sheets and the pages within. It looks like a prop from an old James Bond movie.

I take a deep breath, let it out slowly, and open the cover sheet. On the first page is a big red stamp with a circle. Inside the circle reads TOP SECRET. Underneath this, in bold black caps are the words: SECURITY CLEARANCE REQUIRED. My palms are sweaty. I get up and close the blinds.

I turn to the second page. Centered, in bold black caps, I read aloud: "ENERGENX PROJECT." Then, in smaller print, it states: This information is for those on a *Need-to-Know Basis* only. I think to myself, "Do I need to know?" I answer by turning to the next page. The tiny type is difficult to read, and I realize I'm going to be here for a while.

As I scan the material, my mind spins. It appears to be a military document from the early 1990's detailing a top-secret program that experimented with computer code, particle energy and the world wide web. Even Doctor Who couldn't come up with a scenario like this. From what I can see, the scientists who worked on this project were mavericks, way ahead of their time.

In those days, the internet was in its embryonic stages. The U.S. military began working on the concepts for a computer network for military application in the 1950's and 60's, but the technology was kept secret—the stuff of spy novels. Many other countries, like England and Germany, were developing similar technology. It was during the Cold War. Everyone was afraid of nuking each other and most of this new computer tech was defense related. The first mega-computer mainframes filled whole rooms and personal computing was an invention for the future.

In the 1970's, ARPANET, the first internet network, was established. It was named after ARPA, or the Advanced Research Projects Agency, a division of the U.S. Department of Defense. The mega-computers were designed and built for military use, but eventually research facilities and universities got them, too.

The first computer message was sent through the ARPANET from UCLA to SRI (Stanford Research Institute), right here in Palo Alto. Silicon Valley, a little bit south from us, got its name from the silicon chip, or microprocessor chip, used to run the first small computers. Chips revolutionized the computer industry, to the point where we can look up anything on the tiniest of screens now.

A bunch of awesome geeks were experimenting with computer tech in the late 1980's. It was a new science that attracted some of the most brilliant minds in the country, including my father. The TCP/IP protocol for navigating the ARPANET was developed, and the United States government began to witness the amazing phenomenon taxpayer dollars created. My dad says that the American people paid for the development of the internet, which is now the most powerful tool for free exchange of information ever known to mankind. Then, fifteen years before I was born, my hero, Tim Berners-Lee, introduced the most extraordinary marvel since the printing press: the World Wide Web. And he insisted it be kept free for the people.

I doubt the geeks back then could have predicted where future generations would take their brainchild. My dad's generation included Bill Gates and Steve Jobs, the pioneering founders of Microsoft and Apple. The next generation commercialized the internet and brought us websites like Amazon, E-bay, Facebook, and Twitter. 1980's nerds pioneered technology that helped create 21st century tech billionaires.

Suddenly, I realize I'm gaping into space, reflecting on the history of computers and all the hours Oshi and I spend studying together—the way she always chews on her eraser and I always ask if it tastes good. I rub the spot on my upper arm where she pokes me, but it isn't as sore as it should be. My eyes are moist, and I realize I really miss her. I feel so alone. I turn the lights low, so when Mumsy comes home, she won't know I'm up. I just can't face her, and my sadness, at the same time.

I hear twigs snap in the bushes outside, bringing me out of my melancholia. Inching up to my window, I squint through the blinds, but nothing seems out of the ordinary. No SUV. No hulking maniac. Then, I hear what sounds like a dog going through the garbage cans. I slip out and grab a broom from the hall closet. I'm becoming a Jedi Master with the broom lately. Exiting the front door as ninja-like as possible, I tiptoe slowly to the garbage cans. "Shoo," I say. Instead of an animal growl, I hear an unmistakable giggle.

"Paulie?" I ask.

He jumps out from behind the cans and yells, "Boo!"

I give him the reaction he wants and jump up off the ground. "Dude...you scared the bejezzuz outta me!" I whisper-yell.

Paulie laughs. "I got you. Big time," he declares.

"Yup, you sure did," I say. "What are you doing here? It's after ten. You shouldn't be roaming the neighborhood alone."

"I couldn't sleep, wondering about the document Joe gave you. What's in it?"

"Come on, I'll show you. Just be quiet, ok? Sara's asleep."

"You got it, dude," he whispers. He weaves down the hallway, ahead of me, tiptoeing absurdly. It's all I can do to keep from busting up. In my room, Paulie falls onto the bed. I tell him everything about Detective Ritchie and what I've read in the document so far. We stare at each other. There are no words. This new knowledge weighs on us like an eight-hundred-pound gorilla.

"Take a look at this," I say. Paulie sits at attention as I show him the pages with reports and diagrams recording experiments that took place over a period of two years. He stares at them blankly. "Look!" I emphasize the importance of the diagram by poking my index finger on it. His eyes beg me to explain.

"In this experiment, a chimpanzee was placed in a chamber where its energy field was scanned, harnessed and gathered into a tube! The energy in the tube was then pressurized into a small particle."

Paulie gawks at me.

"You know, like fission? The way they make atom bombs?"

He shakes his head.

Trying to explain nuclear science to Paulie is beyond my level of patience right now, but it's a relief to share this astounding discovery with him, even if he doesn't understand it. I relax a little.

"They were experimenting a lot back then with fission, but I never thought they could apply the scientific principles to computer technology," I say, mostly to myself. I drop the document on my desk and pull up a chair to face Paulie. "So, they took this small particle of energy, which they created through fission, and placed it inside a weapon," I explain, then ask him, "Have you ever seen the movie *Men in Black?*"

"Oh. Yeah! That kind of weapon? No. Frakkin. Way."

"Way," I assure him. "It was proven, that this particle, when shot through the weapon, could make a blast the size of a small atomic bomb. Several tests were carried out in the Pacific Ocean."

"Wowza!" Paulie exclaims. "For real?"

I point to the document on my desk, "Yes, according to that."

"What happened to the chimp?" Paulie asks, genuinely concerned.

"Hmmm…they don't say," I answer. "It's not the chimp that got shot through the weapon, but its energy field. Maybe it generated a new field and went on living. Who knows?"

We're both quiet for a moment mulling this over, then Paulie squirms. "Hey, you got anything to eat? All this thinking is making me hungry."

I ignore him and pick up the document. "This was such futuristic stuff. I feel like I'm reading a Ray Bradbury novel."

There's a *huh?* expression on Paulie's face.

"*Fahrenheit 451? The Illustrated Man? The Martian Chronicles?*"

Paulie shakes his head.

"Never mind." All at once I become aware of how exhausted I am. I drop down onto the bed next to Paulie. "Dude," I say. "You should go home. Mumsy will be here soon, and we're both in enough trouble as it is. Your parents hate me."

"No, they don't, Jake. It's just that…well… I've always been their good little boy, ya know? They just don't know how to deal with my recent behavior."

I nudge his shoulder and get up. "Come on," I say. "I'll fill you in tomorrow, after I have a chance to read the rest of it."

When we reach the front door, Paulie says, "Are you sure you're ok, Jake?"

I'm starting to feel like I may have another friend I can trust, besides Oshi. I take the risk and confide in him, "With each passing minute, I fear I'm losing Oshi forever."

And then Paulie does something amazing—he hugs me.

"Don't worry," he says. "We'll find her tomorrow. I can feel it in my bones."

"Thanks," I say.

From the front stoop I watch him cross our lawn. "You want some company?"

"Nah," he responds. "I'm good."

"Okay, but…text me every minute, ok?" Paulie lives about three minutes away.

"Havva banana," he waves.

"Havva banana," I wave back and watch him walk down the street until he makes a left to the lane where he lives.

It's after eleven and I still haven't found anything in the document leading me to Oshi. I want to fling it across the room, or rip it in two, but fortunately, my fortitude kicks in. I lie down on my bed and make my way through the fine print. I read until I'm bleary-eyed. It's about 1:00AM when I switch off my lamp, grab a flashlight and tuck myself under my blankets with the document—just in case Mumsy catches me up again.

Oshi cries out for me, "Jake! Jake!" I spring to help her. Covered in sweat, I realize I've been dreaming, and the sound of Oshi calling my name is the cawing of crows perched on the trees outside. My toes tug on the blankets, pulling them down off my face. It's barely light out. My head whips around to the clock: 6:32 AM. "Damn!" I say to myself. I grope around in the bed for the document. The flashlight battery has died. So has my phone. I quickly plug it in. It dings. My heart races—Maybe it's Oshi. But it's only Paulie.

Paulie: You up?

Me: Yup.

Paulie: What's the word?

Me: Nothing. Yet.

Paulie: Sorry dude. See you at school.

Me: Not sure. I'll be in touch.

Sara is stirring. I'm acutely aware that there isn't enough time before school to go through page after page of what must be the tiniest print on the planet. Was there a shortage of printer paper in the 90's? I picture some patient secretary, sworn to secrecy, typing every word into one of the first desktop computers and storing it on a floppy disk.

"Focus, focus," I tell myself. I close my eyes to corral some clarity. Several pages of the document slip from my grip and fall to the floor. The few hours I slept wasn't enough. My legs feel like lead as I swing out of bed. Gathering strength, I lean down to pick up the scattered pages. One lying between my feet catches my eye. The heading reads:

Experiment HS-50, Energetic Transportation of Human Subjects

I read the report twice, get up, pace around and take deep breaths to calm myself. It's just too fantastical, too unbelievable. I read it again, out loud, just to make sure I comprehend it: "Human subjects were placed in chambers that scanned their energy field. The energy field was then translated into code, allowing the subjects, physical bodies intact, to enter the network. Two subjects were successfully transmuted. Unfortunately, neither was recovered. Further tests were terminated."

Neither test subject was recovered? Further tests were terminated? What happened to them? They were human beings for God's sake! This can't be real. This is a fantasy in some lunatic scientist's head, just like Joe said.

Lost in a daze, I rub my sore, confused head until my hair stands on end. I catch my reflection in the mirror on the closet door. I look just like my father the day I helped him into the shower. *No, it can't be!* I refuse to be like my father. I must get a hold of myself.

Sara singing in the bathroom jolts me back to reality. I'm

groggy from lack of sleep, but it's time to face the day. Pages from the document are strewn about the bed, floor, and desk. As I pick them up to re-organize them, I notice the last page. It has three signatures on it, with the names typed underneath. The first name doesn't surprise me. It's the professor from Stanford that Joe mentioned, Dr. Ambrose Lavinski, PhD. The second name is harder to read because a brown coffee stain covers the signatures. Peculiarly, as the mind will do under duress, I think about how irresponsible it was of whoever caused the spill. I mean, didn't they realize how precious this document is?

I tilt the blinds to allow sharp sunlight on the document. I almost fall over. There's no mistaking it. Dr. Buckminster Stone's steely signature stares up at me. *Lavinski and Stone???*

I'm anxious to decipher the third name. I hold it up to the sunlight. The stain from the spill also thinned the bottom of this page. I think it may have disintegrated further as I was carrying it home last night. All I can make out is the beginning of a signature—*Dr. J*...and that's it. I could kick myself for not being more careful, but, after all, we *were* being chased by a homicidal maniac.

Still reeling from the shock of seeing Stone's name on the document, I grab my laptop, plop down on my bed, and search "Dr. Ambrose Lavinski". He comes up immediately—*Head of the Department of Paranormal Research at Stanford University*. Why am I not surprised? I must go to Stanford, find Dr. Lavinski and enlist his help—before it's too late.

CHAPTER 18
FUZZY NINJA FEELINGS

We move quietly through our morning ritual lest we wake Mumsy, who always sleeps past eight. I watch Sara pour sugary cereal into her bowl, but I have no appetite.

"Don'tcha ever worry what that stuff is doing to you?" I ask.

Sara raises her eyebrows and looks at me.

"All that sugar you eat." I point to the bowl.

"My blood sugar level is fine." She eyes me testily.

"Yeah, right, like you know." I put the milk back in the fridge.

"You're not eating?" Sara asks. Normally, at breakfast, I'm like a tiger let out of his cage after a week with no food.

"Not this morning," I answer.

"You look a bit…haggard," she says.

"Wow, where'd you learn such a big word?" I tease as I close the cereal box and put it back in the cupboard. "I didn't get much sleep," I add.

"Yeah…didn't think so. Anything important in that document Joe gave you?"

I put her bowl in the sink. "Come on. Let's go."

After locking Mumsy securely in the house, we cut across lawns and driveways to the bus stop. Sara's inquisitive stare is hard to ignore.

"What? Do I have a big zit on my nose or something?" I ask her.

"Jake...no." She giggles. "What did you find out?"

"It was beyond belief," I tell her truthfully.

Her eyes grow as big as two full moons. "What? Why?" she asks.

"I don't have time to get into it, but..." I hesitate. I don't want Sara to know what I'm doing today. I want to protect her from Mumsy's interrogation, and the police, and Aunt June, and...well, everything, at least for now.

"Listen, Sara," I say. "This is huge; bigger than any of us ever imagined, but I'm going to find Oshi, and hopefully today." I see her bus coming. "You better go."

She trots off. "Don't worry, bro. I've got your back." She throws her hand up for an air high-five.

I air high-five her back, and possibly, for the first time, I feel a real sense of some sort of, well..., older brother love for my little sister.

I stand there until Sara's bus pulls away; I want to be sure she doesn't see me make an about-face to the house to coerce Mumsy into giving me a note for school. I can't send up anymore red flags for Principal Becker.

It's 7:20 am when I unlock the front door. School starts in ten minutes. I'm going to have to wake Mumsy, which isn't a pleasant prospect. It's an "only in an emergency" rule...but this is an emergency, as far as I'm concerned. I stride down the hallway and gently open her door.

"Mumsy?" She's sound asleep, limbs akimbo, pillow over her head to keep out morning light and sounds. I walk to the side of the bed, lightly touch her shoulder, and speak softly, "Mumsy?"

She jumps and throws off the pillow. "What? Huh? Jake? Is everything all right?" She starts to get up and put her clothes on.

"It's ok, Mumsy. Calm down. It's not the hospital." I gently push her back onto the bed. "I'm sorry to wake you, but I need an excuse for school. It's really important."

She rubs her forehead. "What? Why didn't you leave a note for me last night? What's all this about?"

For one tortured moment, I decide to tell her, just get the whole thing off my chest. I feel the relief of having an adult to share this with before I even open my mouth—but instantly, I change my mind. I need to wait, just one more day.

"I only found out when I woke up," I lie. *One last time*, I rationalize to myself. "I got a text from Vlad saying there's a career fair going on at Kabam today, and he invited me to go with him. It might be a good place for me to apply for a summer job." I know the *summer job* part of that sentence will motivate her.

"Ok, Jake, but this better be real. You're already in a lot of trouble at school." Still half asleep, she reaches for her official prescription pad on the nightstand and scribbles.

"Thanks, Mumsy." I take the note and fold it.

She lies back down with a sigh. "I'm glad you woke me. It was the smart thing to do."

As I stuff the note in my pocket I'm surprised by that fuzzy, warm feeling again. I turn back to look at Mumsy, catching those last few Z's before she must face another day of work.

"Mumsy?"

"Yeah, Jake," she says sleepily, her face squished by the pillows.

"Thanks for all you do." I feel my face flush as this sentiment hangs heavily in the air.

Mumsy could overreact, overwhelmed by this expression of gratitude from her formerly unappreciative teenager, but thankfully, she doesn't. "No problem, Jake. It's my job, making sure you guys are ok. That's what parents do."

I linger a moment, basking in the warmth of her affection. It may be a moment too long. She props herself up on her elbows. "Are you ok, Jake?"

I snap to. "Yeah, yeah. Sure. I better get going or I'll be late." I smile reassuringly and walk out the door.

Of course, my bus is long gone. Luckily, I catch a ride with some similarly late classmates. In the office, I hand the secretary my note. She looks questioningly at it, but it *is* on Mumsy's prescription pad after all. I feel exhilarated leaving the school knowing I'm on a mission of life or death, while hundreds of my peers are stuck in boring classes.

An unusual sense of elation fills me as I walk towards the city bus that will transport me to Stanford University. I feel like I have a real purpose, maybe for the first time in my life. Men and women in business suits, some wearing tennis shoes, stride swiftly past. I increase my pace to match theirs. Once on the bus they bury their noses in newspapers or cell phones. Propped in a corner seat, I observe passengers get on and off while we pass though the quaint 1920's architecture of downtown Palo Alto. Outside, a man with food on his apron places a sandwich board on the sidewalk in front of his delicatessen. An old-fashioned barber shop sports a red, white, and blue spinning pole. A woman waves incense around a homeless man who has taken up residence on the stoop of her sari shop. Bunches of roses, tulips and daisies spill over a cart pushed by a turbaned man. I take it all in. It feels so new to me, this bus ride through downtown, *and* the peace that I feel. I think of my computer game, *Ninja Warriors*. Could this be what a real Ninja feels like? I laugh out loud. People stare, but I don't care. A toddler on his mother's lap grins goofily at me. I gaze at him and think, "You feel me, don'tcha?"

I'm jolted out of my metaphysical mood when the bus jerks to a stop and I realize we're in front of Stanford University. I jump up as the bus doors start to close and push my hand between the rubber to force them open. The little boy, an innocent smile on his face, twiddles his fingers at me. I twiddle back and hop onto the sidewalk.

I'd forgotten how immense the Stanford grounds are. My dad's an alumnus, so my chances of getting into Stanford are good. I'm daydreaming about Oshi and me, hand in hand, strolling across campus, when suddenly, some jerk on a bicycle practically knocks me over, and then yells, "Hey, airhead, watch where the hell you're walking!" I'm too stunned to think of anything to yell back, so I shake my fist at him instead. From the nearby grassy slope, a group of students watches me brandish my fifteen-year-old fist at an upper classman. Embarrassed, I slowly put my hands in the pockets of my jeans and try to act like I belong here.

It seems like I cover acres of campus on my way to find Dr. Lavinski. With so much impressive architecture—Stanford was built in 1885—I'm almost certain I'm going to find him in a Harry Potter-like castle. I'm disappointed when I see the sign for The Department of Paranormal Research embedded on a rectangular, 1960's, one-story building. Students scurry past as I stand transfixed, staring at the sign. *This is it—my last chance to find Oshi.*

I plunge into the river of college kids entering the building.

I must appear strangely out-of-place as I search for Dr. Lavinski's department. A cute girl with dreads and black horn-rimmed glasses approaches me. "Are you looking for something?" she asks me as she switches a load of books from one hip to the other.

I feel my face grow hot. I'm embarrassed to ask about the Paranormal Research Department. She'll think I'm a weirdo for sure. I prep myself to sound confident, but before I get the words out, she says, "I bet you're looking for the Paranormal Lab, huh? They couldn't make it harder to find, could they?" A huge, gorgeous smile adorns her face, putting me at ease.

"Yeah, ha ha!" I laugh way too loudly.

"Follow me," she says.

Feeling awkward, I follow her as we snake through a hallway of students rushing to class. She stops at an opening with no door and points down. "Here ya go, kiddo", confirming my suspicion that she's aware I don't belong here.

"Thanks," I say.

"No prob. See ya," she says and leaves me staring down a dimly lit, narrow concrete stairwell leading to an unadorned, thick metal door at the bottom that screams: *You're not getting in here, buddy.* I step toward the unknown.

CHAPTER 19
IS THIS FOR REAL?

It's hemmed in here at the bottom of the stairwell: just me and the old metal door that looks like it could belong in a parking garage. There is no handle, only a dead bolt. The BAM BAM of my knocking echoes in the confined space. I put my ear to the cold metal, but what am I thinking? Like I could hear through galvanized steel?

I bang again, "Hello? Is anybody in there?" I yell. A few more attempts and I'm worn out. I sit down on the bottom step and lean my head against the cool concrete wall. My vision blurs as I stare into space, wondering how I'm going to find Dr. Lavinski.

I'm suddenly jarred by loud footsteps at the top of the stairwell. Six people in white lab coats charge down the stairs like a herd of caribou. I stand up. They barely notice me.

"Let me pass, let me pass," says a gravelly voice, thick with an Eastern European accent. A stooped, white-haired man, with Coke-bottle-bottom glasses and a white goatee, pushes through the group, keys jangling from his right hand. In his left is a notebook. The lab assistants stand aside to let him through. He swooshes past me, puts a key into the deadbolt, then stops and faces me. The name stitched on his lab coat says Dr. Ambrose Lavinski.

"What are you doing down here, young man?" he asks me in a tone that isn't unkind. Five pairs of eyes lock onto me.

"Dr. Lavinski?" I ask, feeling stupid. It's right there on his nametag, after all.

"Yes, it is I." He smiles. "What might I do for you?"

Between the eyes boring into me and this restrictive space, I'm beginning to feel claustrophobic. I clear my throat, but what comes out sounds jittery, even to me. "Uh, sir…is there somewhere we can talk, in private?" The eyes turn to Dr. Lavinski, as if I am a lab experiment. He unlocks the door and waves the group in ahead of him.

The heavy door closes with a perceptible *whoosh. What is behind that door?* I pull the document from my backpack and hand it to Dr. Lavinski. There's nothing to do but wait as he scans it, but the recognition comes within seconds. He looks at me over the top of his glasses and asks, "Just where did you come by this?"

"It's a long story, sir," I reply.

"Hmmm. Then, you must come in," he says, unlocking the door again. "Just remember…what you see here, stays here. You got it?"

I nod.

"Well, then, follow me."

Whoosh, the door closes behind me. I tentatively step into the lab. What I see before me is incredible…no…magical. It's a place that normally exists only in the imagination, or in films with a large special effects budget. It's a huge, open laboratory, about the size of a tennis court. On one side of the room are large, rectangular, glass tanks filled with water. Human subjects float peacefully, wires attached to their heads and masks over their nose and mouth.

On the other side of the room are glass-walled enclosures, not unlike the practice rooms in the music department at school. Outside the glass rooms, lab-coated researchers hover over computer monitors and other intricate instruments. In one of the enclosures, a chimp romps playfully. A middle-aged woman, wires running from her head to the instruments, sits in a high, comfortable chair outside the room, facing the glass. I want to stop and watch, but Dr. Lavinski walks briskly, his attention focused straight ahead. As we pass by the enclosure, the romping chimp disappears. I stop dead. *What the….???*

Dr. Lavinski, his back to me, waves his arm in a big circle and says, "Come along, son."

I stumble and catch up to him. "But, but…Dr. Lavinski!" I say, much louder than I need to. "Did you see that? That monkey. Am I crazy?"

"Chimpanzee," he corrects me. "No, you are not crazy."

We're passing by a bulky, futuristic pod in the middle of the laboratory. It's at least ten feet high and shaped like a rocket. Surrounding this menagerie of instruments, tanks, and the pod, are at least fifty computer monitors hanging from the ceiling and the walls. They display graphics and reports as well as real-time videos of events taking place in the lab. I want to touch everything, experiment, immerse myself in it. It's like visiting Disneyland and being dragged past the rides.

We're heading toward the back of the lab. A large cage with bushes and boulders houses several chimps who eat figs and lounge comfortably. An opening leads outside to a jungle-themed enclosure. The chimps pant and hoot when they see Dr. Lavinski. He waves at them and they jump up and down excitedly.

"Not now, my friends," he says, and then orders a nearby lab assistant, "Get them more figs!" The chimps whoop with delight.

Privacy doesn't exist in this place. Every wall is glass. It's kind of cool, but spooky too. The lights are kept low, which casts an eerie pall. Dr. Lavinski guides me into his office, a glass cubicle in the back corner. We will be seen, but not heard. He shuts the door and sits down behind his desk, then motions for me to sit opposite him. He sets the tattered document between us on the desk, leans back and crosses his fingers behind his head.

Minutes pass as Dr. Lavinski stares at me, bug-eyed through his thick glasses. I fidget in my seat. "So?" He finally asks in his thick accent. "What is it you want to discuss with me?"

I take the flash drive with the enhanced videos of Oshi out of my backpack and hand it to Dr. Lavinski. His big, hairy eyebrows lift. "Don't worry, they're short," I say.

He inserts the flash drive into the port on his laptop and clicks play. I can't see, but it doesn't matter. I've watched so many times, I mouth Oshi's words, "Help me. I'm stuck in here."

"What is she saying?" Dr. Lavinski asks, concerned. "She looks terrified."

"That's my friend, Oshi O'Malley," I answer. "She's stuck in there and she's begging for help."

Dr. Lavinski's eyes search mine for an explanation. "Stuck? In where?"

"The web," I say, like I'm talking about the weather.

"What web?" he asks, sounding a bit perturbed.

"The World Wide Web," I answer.

He shrinks back, sitting up, realization sinking in. I feel like this shouldn't be too far of a stretch for the man who invented the technology almost 30 years ago. I scootch my chair closer to the desk and lean across, keeping my voice low. "The hacker who told me about you, Joe Porter, analyzed this on his high-end gear—you know, digital spectrum analyzers, voice recognition, equalizers, phasers and filters... "

Dr. Lavinski regards me over his glasses. I realize I sound like a love-struck teenager talking about Joe's equipment.

"Bah...this could be a prank, no?" he asks, angering me.

"Well, yeah...I guess it could," I answer, more tersely than I'd like. "But it's not, because she's been missing for over forty-eight hours and no one knows where she is. And now the police are looking too. A cop came to see me. I lied to him—said I didn't know anything. I don't feel good about that."

"I see," he says, thoughtfully. "And so, now will you reveal the reason you are here and how you came upon this?" He taps the document.

"Joe told me about you. He gave me the document," I say.

"Hmmm...Joe...um...Porter, you say? Doesn't ring a bell."

"I only met him two days ago. One thing's for sure, he's a stellar hacker. I figure he's hiding from the government for cracking into top-secret programs for that billionaire scumbag, Buckminster Stone, and..."

Dr. Lavinski slams his palm on the desk, and I flinch. "Stone," he says under his breath, glaring out towards the lab. I follow his gaze, but no one has noticed his outburst.

"Right?" I concur. "That guy is evil."

"You don't know the half of it," he adds, his face steely.

"Both of your names are on that," I say, nodding toward the document. My words have an accusatory tone that I wish I could take back.

I wait for a reaction, but Dr. Lavinski remains stoic so I continue, "Have you heard of Stone Micro Dynamics, his company? I went there because Joe said Stone might be involved with Oshi's disappearance. I thought I might find out something useful, but instead he threatened to call security." I pause, waiting for Dr. Lavinski to take it all in. He motions for me to continue. "I told Stone who my dad is and how he trained me to code better than any of his lame programmers. That shut him up."

"What did you just say?" Dr. Lavinski asks.

"What?"

"You haven't told me your name, son."

"Oh, yeah, sorry. It's Jake, Jake Green."

Dr. Lavinski stares at me, bewildered, and his words come out very slowly. "And what is your father's name?"

"Justin...Dr. Justin Green."

CHAPTER 20
AN INCREDIBLY BRIGHT BOY

I'm expecting a fanfare of recognition, but, instead, Dr. Lavinski leans back in his chair as though the mention of my father's name means nothing to him.

"You must have heard of my father...," I say.

"I may have, yes," he says cagily, and then changes course abruptly. "So, Jake Green, what happened next?" In a manner that says: *Let's get on with it, shall we?*

I'm eager to get on with it too, every minute counting. "After that, Stone went all black-ops on us." The wrinkles on Dr. Lavinski's forehead crease. "Yeah, he brought in his gang of ex-military elite to kidnap Joe. I just happened to be at Joe's apartment when it happened."

Dr. Lavinski's bushy eyebrows raise again.

"They took poor Joe and ripped out all of his hardware." I shudder at the memory. "I was hiding in the hall closet, nearest to Stone, when Joe says, 'It was those kids, they know something' and, right then, Stone steps to the closet door, like he knew I was there, and says, 'I'll deal with them later.' I thought I was gonna lose it...seriously." Dr. Lavinski looks concerned as he nods for me to continue. "After Stone's men took Joe, Stone says to his last goon, a huge hulk with a jagged scar, 'Take care of this place. Torch it if you have to.'"

"You can't be serious!" Dr. Lavinski exclaims.

"Yes!" I exclaim back. "Stone was gonna burn the place down."

"O Boże. On jest potworem. Prawdziwie." Dr. Lavinski says softly in what must be his native language.

"Huh?"

"A monster…" he explains in English.

"My sister Sara, and my friend Paulie, were there with me. Fortunately, we got out alive, but now I live in fear. I see his black SUV everywhere. I really think he wants to kill me!

Dr. Lavinski leans in, elbows on the desk. "This all sounds very dangerous to me, Jake." A mop of white hair falls into his eyes and he brushes it back.

"I know, I know," I say. "I should be talking to the cops." I rub my sweaty palms furiously on my pant legs as if hoping to scrub away some of the guilt I'm feeling. I push off from my chair and pace the room. "I haven't even told my parents! Don't you see? It's my fault!" I suddenly feel like I need some air, but there isn't any to be had in this square test tube. The lies and secrets of the past few days tumble out of me like a bag of oranges dropped on the sidewalk. "It's my fault Oshi's missing. I infected her boyfr…Sean Haggerty's laptop with a virus…and she's paying for it!" I can feel my voice rising uncontrollably and my pulse quickening.

"It was a stupid, stupid thing to do," I berate myself as I clip back and forth, completely oblivious to how I must look. "I did it because I was jealous, okay? And now, Oshi's been kidnapped or…worse. Stone's got her in the Gotchu site and I don't know how that's even possible, and I didn't believe it myself until I read about *your* similar experiments in *that* document!" I point at him and then the papers on the desk. My hand is shaking.

Dr. Lavinski comes over and puts an arm around my shoulder. He gently guides me back to my chair. "Call me Ambrose," he says.

I finally let go of the fear and frustration I've been holding onto. "I've got to find her and bring her back safely," I sob, tears running down my cheeks. And that's why I'm here, Dr. Lavin…Ambrose."

He brings me a cool glass of water from the 5-gallon bottle in the corner. "Here, drink this," he says. He sits back down in his chair with a sigh, then takes off his thick glasses and lays them on the desk. Ambrose leans in closer, maybe to see me more clearly. His demeanor and tone are serious. "First of all, Jake," he begins. "There is only one way this extraordinary event could have occurred."

He's got my full attention.

"A harmful virus was created by Stone, using the computer code from this experiment." He taps the document.

"You mean this stuff is for real?" I ask.

He nods. "But Stone's Gotchu website isn't."

"I know. Please go on," I implore him.

"From what you have told me, Jake, I believe the Gotchu website was fabricated by Stone for his own diabolical purposes. I hypothesize this is what happened." Ambrose puts his glasses back on, grabs a black marker and stands up. On a nearby Plexiglas board, he draws a large square and scribbles a big G in the middle of it. He stabs at it with the marker. "Gotchu," he explains, "where Stone's virus originated." On the opposite side of the board, he draws a smaller square. "And this," he says, "is what-his-name's laptop."

"Sean's," I say.

"Yes," he says. He puts a large S in the middle of Sean's laptop. "And so…" Ambrose grabs a red marker and draws a line from the Gotchu square to the Sean square. "Stone's Gotchu virus infects Sean's laptop."

Ambrose then places a rectangle in between the Gotchu square and the Sean square and labels it J. "For you, Jake," he offers, but I already had that one figured out. He picks up a yellow marker and slashes lines, like rays of the sun, from my rectangle through the red line and explains, "In some strange anomaly, the viral code you created for Sean's laptop intercepts Stone's Gotchu virus." He circles the red line with the yellow marker, then uses both the red and yellow markers to draw one line to Sean's laptop.

I look at him quizzically, elbows on the desk, palms under my chin.

"Don't you see? It is the only plausible explanation," he says, as though I'm a dimwitted student. "This Gotchu virus wasn't just meant for Sean's laptop, Jake. It was meant for millions of laptops; for anybody who happened upon an enticing pop-up box that afternoon. An invitation which contained a dangerous virus, which your *friend*…"—he winks at me and I feel my cheeks flush—"…naturally, out of curiosity…clicked on. There is no way she could have known, Jake. And that's exactly what Stone was counting on, millions of people clicking on that box."

I feel numb.

"But, unbeknownst to him," he waggles the markers at me, "an incredibly bright boy created his own special viral code—the Revenge Virus, shall we call it?" He returns to the board, taps the J rectangle several times. "The Revenge Virus intercepts the incredibly evil Gotchu virus! And, *BAM!* Like white blood cells surrounding an invading virus in the human body, no?" Ambrose drags the markers from the J square and stabs them into the center of the S square. "The Gotchu virus gets contained onto Sean's hard drive. His computer must have been the only one on the planet with the Gotchu virus when Oshi unsuspectingly clicked on the enticing pop-up box. Unbelievable? Perhaps. But entirely possible."

Finished, he tosses the markers with flourish onto his desk. "Mr. Jake Green," he states emphatically, "you are, in fact, a hero!" Ambrose gets himself a glass of water and drinks thirstily.

Silence fills the room. I look out into the lab. Researchers, equipment, computers, chimps…yep…it's all still there. I'm shaking uncontrollably. What Ambrose just explained hasn't changed a thing. Oshi's still missing.

"This Gotchu pop-up box," I say quietly, "It was still on Sean's computer when I took it home. I clicked on it, but it just took me to the innocent looking Gotchu social site. I signed up and then the videos of Oshi started coming through."

"Stone must have followed your code back to you and realized his plans had been foiled. Oh, but he's got Oshi alright, and he's sending you those videos. You are very brave to stand-up to this wicked madman, Jake."

"I don't feel brave. So I created a virus which accidentally intercepted some lunatic's hellish plan."

"You are a genius, Jake, just like…" he stops.

I blush. That kind of compliment used to feed my ego, but

right now I feel only sadness and shame. "I'm good, I guess... but obviously not good enough to save my best friend."

"Jake," he says, more businesslike. "What's the expression people use these days?" He looks up at the ceiling as if there's an English slang dictionary inscribed up there. "Ah...I've got it: Stop beating yourself up."

"But I have to do something!" I snatch the document and shake it at Ambrose. "What about all this incredible stuff you did? I need to get to Oshi! You can help me...can't you?"

"Come on," he says. "I want to show you something." I feel fatigued, but I rise with him. At this point, Dr. Ambrose Lavinski, one of the leading paranormal scientists in the world, is my last and only hope.

CHAPTER 21
A MIND BLOWN

It's refreshing to escape the confines of Ambrose's glass box and the emotions expressed there. Over the noise of the chimps, I ask Ambrose, "Can you help me or not?"

Ambrose doesn't answer for as long as it takes us to walk to the glass enclosures with the test subjects. I look up at the clock on the wall, astonished to see that I've only been here for an hour. Ambrose faces me, out of earshot of the students. He takes off his glasses and cleans them on his lab coat.

"Jake," I hear reluctance in his voice, and for the first time I'm truly afraid. Afraid that he won't be able to help me or doesn't want to. I'll never be able to find Oshi, my life in ruins. My mind skip jumps to a future of scrounging food out of dumpsters and keeping warm by the fire under an overpass. Ambrose's voice jolts me back into the lab.

"Jake," he pulls me closer to him and speaks quietly. "Someone—most likely Stone—used the code we invented, the one used in the experiments in the document, without authorization. At the end of the project, the three scientists involved signed a confidentiality agreement promising that we would never speak about that code again. I'm forbidden to use it. Do you understand? It would affect my university position and my research here. My life, and that of my family, could even be in danger." He puts his glasses back on and waves a hand at me. "Besides, we weren't allowed to keep a copy of the code and I don't remember it. It was extremely complex, as you must know."

"Well, maybe it's more complicated than string theory or dark matter, but obviously Stone has remembered it or gotten access to it somehow, or the virus wouldn't have dumped Oshi into the World Wide Web!" I realize my volume has increased, and Ambrose glances around, annoyed.

"Please, Jake, I want to help you, I really do, but we must be discreet."

I nod, compliant. "Sorry, doc."

Ambrose strolls to the glass room with the frolicking chimp. Despite my raw nerves, I'm excited to find out what's happening with this experiment. Ambrose steps over to the older woman I saw earlier who sits outside the enclosure. "Hello, Miriam," he says.

She opens her eyes slowly, as if coming out of a trance. "Hello," she says sleepily.

"This is Jake," Ambrose says.

"Hello, Jake," Miriam says.

I hold my hand up in a friendly gesture, still perplexed about what's going on.

"I'm going to explain to Jake what you're doing with Gertrude, our chimp," Ambrose says to Miriam. She nods. He turns to me, "Miriam is able to transfer energy using her mind. Are you aware that the average human uses only 10 percent of his or her brain matter?"

I nod. "Any intelligent kid knows that."

Ambrose continues, "Miriam is simply tapping into a small portion of the other 90 percent, an area that interfaces with energy fields—sometimes referred to as *auras*. Miriam uses psychic skills that most of the human population doesn't believe in, let alone acknowledge. But all of us are capable of it. Do you believe what I'm saying, Jake?"

"I, uh…I don't know…I guess so?" I stammer.

"How about if we prove it to you…scientifically?" he asks.

"Sure," I answer, not sounding so sure.

"Ok, then," he says, motioning to Miriam. "Whenever you want to begin."

Miriam adjusts herself on her chair, checks the nodules on her head, then nods to the researchers huddled over their monitors. She closes her eyes and appears to be concentrating. On one monitor, I see a graph that spikes up and down. "That monitor shows her brain wave activity," says Ambrose. My eyes dart between Miriam, the chimp, and the monitors, taking it all in.

"Keep your eyes on Gertrude," Ambrose whispers to me.

I watch the chimp peeling its banana as I steal glances at the monitor. Miriam's brain waves look like a mountain range; up and down, but mostly spiked peaks on the graph. I look back at Gertrude, but nothing's happening. Ambrose holds his hand out in a low gesture that implies, *wait for it.* Suddenly, Gertrude disappears!

I'm stunned speechless. I look around for someone to share this amazing moment with, but it's business as usual in the lab—no one reacts. I, on the other hand, want to scream and jump! I wish Paulie and Sara and…Oshi…were here to see this. How will I ever explain it to them?

Ambrose leans over and says to me, "Now, watch this." He presses a button on the enclosure. Instantly, a whitish/yellow aura that looks like a chimp's body appears inside the glass room. The aura transforms into a sparkling, multi-colored, three-dimensional hologram. I'm watching a rainbow-colored energy field peel and eat a banana. With a twinkle in his eye, Ambrose releases the button and *poof*! Gertrude is gone again.

I want to say I blink and wipe my eyes, like they do in the movies, but I just keep staring at the empty space where Gertrude used to be.

"Well, Jake, what do you think of that?" Ambrose prods me with his elbow.

"I...uh...," I step back from the window and look at the brain wave graph again. It isn't spiking anymore, instead, the line is riding very high on the screen with only slight dips—a rolling landscape instead of the Himalayas.

"Props, doc! That is amazing!" I say loudly, forgetting myself.

"Would you like to see Gertrude reappear?" he asks me, the tone in his voice not unlike a carnie at the county fair, enticing people to enter the hall of mirrors.

What am I gonna say? *Nah, that's ok, doc. I don't care whether I witness one of the most unbelievable phenomena I've... hey, hardly anybody for that matter...has ever seen.* Of course I want to see Gertrude reappear! My head bobs enthusiastically.

Ambrose puts a gentle hand on Miriam's shoulder, "Okay, Miriam, reintegration." I glance at the graph, which now displays the very spiky, mountainous line again. My eyes search the glass room for Gertrude. Suddenly, she reappears, sitting on the floor, chewing on a leaf.

"Wow," I say, mesmerized, my eyes glued on Gertrude. She looks up at me through the glass and hoots.

"This is just one of the phenomena that we research and evaluate here," Ambrose says. "It's all recorded and documented for posterity, but, unfortunately, not for the scientific journals… yet."

I sense disappointment in Ambrose's voice. "Why not?" I ask.

Ambrose answers, "The general populace isn't ready for this view of reality." Facing me, he places his palm on my shoulder. "Do you know the story of the first explorers arriving in the New World?"

"You mean like how we started eating turkey and stuff?" I ask.

He laughs and removes his hand. "When the foreign ships arrived on the coast of North America, the indigenous Natives could not see the ships because they were a phenomenon they had never witnessed before. Although the work we do here is scientifically valid, people's belief systems override the facts." He speaks to Miriam. "Thank you." She nods, eyes closed, probably off using some other part of the 90 percent of her brain that most of us will never access.

"What you're doing here…it's just so…mind-blowing," I sound gushy again.

"Important work, yes, thank you," he says. He begins walking, hands clasped behind him, and I follow. When we reach the giant pod in the middle of the lab, he stops and gazes up at it. No one is near the pod, and it seems that no experiments are in process.

"What is this?" I ask.

Ambrose crosses his arms in front of his chest and bows his head. "I'm deliberating, Jake, whether I should tell you something or not."

"Tell me what?"

Slowly raising his head, he taps his cheek with his index finger and stares at the pod. "Hmm, hmm, hmm," he murmurs, then steps over to a bank of computers nearby and pushes a few buttons. I can hear a slight whir and a couple of beeps. I join him at the controls, pacing in small circles while he pushes keys and adjusts knobs. I can't begin to imagine what he's doing. The pod emits a low rumble. Finally, he speaks. "I may know how to retrieve your friend." He says this so quietly I barely hear him.

I stop my pacing. "What? How? Please tell me!" I yell-whisper.

A commotion begins in the pod as Ambrose continues to play with the controls. There is a whirring sound, and a multicolored mist begins to rise and spin around. My mouth hangs open.

"This," Ambrose says, pointing up. "But we would need the code."

A few lab personnel stop what they're doing and look towards the pod. I assume they don't get to see it powered up very often. A couple of them begin to saunter over but Ambrose motions for them to remain at their stations. Disappointment shows on their faces, but they do as they're told. Ambrose powers down the pod.

I must look like that kid in Charlie and the Chocolate Factory who just got the golden ticket, mouth agape, eyes as wide as saucers.

"Jake. Jake?" Ambrose tries to get my attention.

"Yeah, the code," I answer.

"Do you know that military base near here, right off the interstate?"

"Yeah," I say. "My dad used to take us to air shows there."

"I believe the code which could transport you into the World Wide Web to find your friend, is stored there." He says this matter-of-factly, like transporting a human being into the web is as normal as driving to the store for a carton of milk. He continues, "There is a commonplace bunker there, a very unobtrusive structure."

I'm elated, and frightened, at the same time.

"But...," he says.

"Yeah?" I ask.

"It wouldn't be without risk, Jake," he answers. "The bunker I speak of is actually a storage facility for old, classified military information. One must have top-secret security clearance to attain access. His eyes search the lab for any possibility of being overheard. "Come on," he grabs my arm and whisks me back to his office.

I figure by now there must be a few curious lab assistants wondering what the heck Ambrose and I are up to, but no one seems to scrutinize us skulking about. As the door closes to possible interlopers Ambrose points to the document still sitting on his desk and says, "These three people have clearance."

"And...?" I ask.

"My clearance can get you, and your friends, through the security checkpoint."

I flop into the chair. "Great. Three kids scurrying around a top-security military installation. *That* won't be obvious."

"Look around you," he says. "You have seen a small sampling of what is at my disposal. Now, I suggest that you go home and get some rest and meet me at the downtown bus stop at sunset. I will have everything prepared for you. I can't accompany you into the bunker, but I will make sure you get onto the base and that you remain safe!"

CHAPTER 22

COORDINATING THE TEAM

It's hard to sleep when it's light out. I shut the blinds, put the pillow over my head, and drift into a fitful rest, the lucid land between wake and sleep. Oshi is in my bedroom, floating near the ceiling. She's laughing, then crying, then cackling like a witch, taunting me. An oily, black substance oozes from her mouth and ears and morphs into bulbous, ominous-looking creatures that pull on her arms and legs. She cries out. I jump up from the bed and swipe at the creatures with my pillow, but it just sails through them like ice through water. They turn on me and push me back onto the bed. They pull on my arms and legs as if to draw and quarter me. It hurts and I'm screaming with my legs and arms spread eagle. Off in the distance, I hear Sara's voice, "Jake, Jake..." I squirm to free myself as I strain to follow her voice. Then her hand is on my shoulder, shaking me.

"Jake! Jake! Wake up! You're having a nightmare...no, a daymare...I don't know. Is there such a thing?"

I'm delusional. I throw the pillows off and look up at the ceiling, realizing I've been dreaming. The events of the morning come rushing back to me. I look at the clock. It's 4:10PM. Sara must have just come home from dance class.

I search for my phone and text Paulie: Where are you?

I say to Sara. "We have to go. Get out of those pink tights and grab some Ninja clothes."

She doesn't move.

"Do you wanna help me find Oshi, or not?" I ask her.

"Well, of course, but can you give me a little bit more to go on here?"

My phone notifies me of a text.

Paulie: Just got home. Where are you? Did you cut school again?

Me: More on that later. Coming to get you. We have a mission tonight.

Paulie: Sounds cool. All in bro.

Me: Wear black. Dress warm. Bring a ski mask.

I motion for Sara to get ready. Her eyebrows are pinched.

"Don't worry," I say. "We'll be safe. I can take you to a friend's house if you want, but I don't want Mumsy to know where I'm going. It's better if you're with me. Plus, I could use your support." I manage a reassuring smile for her.

"Ok." She surrenders and goes off to her room to change.

"Remember," I yell. "Wear black."

I scribble a note for Mumsy:

Dear Mumsy,
In case you come home before we do, don't worry. Sara is safe with me. We're on a mission. Someone's life may be in danger. You just have to trust me. I'll text you later.

Love, Jake

An hour later the three of us are on the bus to meet Ambrose. We snuck up to Paulie's parents' car at the deli and left a note because, odds are, Paulie won't be home until very late. This could mean a long stint of restriction, like never being able to leave his house again, but he says it's worth it.

"You two aren't afraid, are ya?" I ask Sara and Paulie as the bus bumps along. We are sitting in the very back so we can talk freely.

"Like I said, all in, bro," Paulie answers.

Sara is quiet, staring out the window.

"Sara? Are you having second thoughts?" I ask her. "Because it's still ok for you to turn back. You don't have to come."

Sara plucks at a loose thread on her sleeve. "I was just thinking about Mumsy," she gulps back a little cry. "When she reads the note."

I put my arm around my sister, "I know, I know. She'll be worried, but I'm hoping she feels better knowing you're with me."

We look into each other's eyes for a long moment and then burst out laughing at the absurdity of what I just said. Paulie is oblivious to what's funny but becomes infected with our mirth. The three of us can't stop laughing, even though the passengers up front glare at us. I wipe tears from my eyes. "Stop, stop." I hold up my hand. "You *can* trust me, Sara…really," I say.

Sara slaps my thigh. "I know, big brother." And that seems to take care of the tension we're feeling about Mumsy, and maybe about this evening as well. It's no secret that we're all apprehensive, but after Joe's apartment, where we brought down a 250-pound gorilla-man, I have total confidence in our dynamic trio.

I motion for them to lean in. "I saw some seriously unbelievable stuff today at Ambrose's lab. I really wish you could have seen it. He's going to help us. Our mission might be a bit dangerous, but we're going to find Oshi tonight, I just know it!"

Ambrose is waiting in his black Mercedes at the bus stop. He gestures for us to get in. I make the necessary introductions and then it's down to business. As he drives, Ambrose explains a few things.

"As I told Jake earlier, I won't be accompanying you into the facility. However, I have brought along some highly advanced technology to help you on your mission."

I sit in the front with Ambrose who is driving like an absent-minded professor. I try to stay focused on what he's saying, but I also want to tell him that red means stop.

Ambrose continues, "I will park outside the fence and wait for you. The fence is electrified."

"Electrified?" Paulie asks.

Ambrose answers, "Yes, but don't worry. I have brought tech for any situation that may arise."

Paulie turns to Sara and says sarcastically, "Well, that's a comfort."

I give Paulie the evil eye and say to Ambrose, "Thanks. We really appreciate everything you are risking to make this happen for us."

"Most certainly, Jake. I do want to help, at least to the degree that I am able."

We're in the fast lane on the freeway as the sun sets to the west. An air strip appears on our left and Ambrose takes the next exit. We drive through a seedy neighborhood that appears to be old military housing. Only a few of the houses look inhabited. Ambrose says, "A result of President Clinton's closure of military bases back in 1993."

"Uh…do you think we're safe driving around here in this expensive Mercedes?" Paulie asks. "I mean, it's kind of sketch around here and…" He stops short when I turn and glare at him again.

Shortly, we come to a deserted playground. The equipment is old and dilapidated. A feral-looking cat covers its poop in the sandbox, then scurries away. Ambrose pulls into the parking lot as the last vestiges of sunlight dip below the horizon.

"Hand me that black bag under your feet, Paulie," Ambrose says. Paulie does as he's told. Ambrose unzips the bag, removes a small stainless steel box, and opens it carefully. A tiny injection needle sits delicately on a piece of foam.

"Jake, can you move closer to me please?" Ambrose asks. "I'm going to inject a microchip behind your ear. This is how you and I will communicate. Also, it will GPS your coordinates to me and to the lab." *Trust, Jake, trust*, I remind myself.

"Sure, doc," I say, as I edge closer to him. He folds my left earlobe forward and presses the tiny needle against the skin behind my ear.

"It will only hurt a little bit," he says, and smiles that mad-scientist grin of his. "It's better if you relax, Jake. Take a few deep breaths."

And, *FWHAP!* As I'm exhaling the first breath, he injects me. It hurts like hell.

"As of this moment, your every movement, what you feel, see, hear, and your vitals, like blood pressure and heart rate, are being monitored by a few trusted people back at the lab." He restores the needle to the container and snaps it shut.

Sara flexes over the front seat. "Are you ok, Jake?"

I rub my neck. "Yeah, I'm fine. It only hurts a little, like he said." I grimace.

Suddenly, Ambrose asks more seriously, "Are you all ready?" He eyes each one of us in turn. We do the same, then nod our heads in unison. "Ok," Ambrose says. "Let's go."

Ambrose backs the car out of the lot and drives down the street of run-down homes. Between this backdrop and the microchip imbedded behind my ear, I'm really starting to feel like a secret agent. If I wasn't so worried about Oshi, I might actually be enjoying myself.

The housing project disappears into a vast field surrounded by electric fencing, the kind that has circular spiky steel wire on top. In the distance I can vaguely make out a guard station. My stomach lurches as I realize what we are about to do. Ambrose stops the car. The sun has set, and darkness cloaks us. "Come on," he says and gets out.

"What are we doing?" Paulie asks.

"I don't know. Just do as he says, please," I answer.

Ambrose walks around to the back and opens the trunk. "Come, come." He hurries us with a wave of his arm. "We are approaching the high-security section of the base. I will need my clearance to get us in."

Sara and Paulie look to me for reassurance. I motion for them to get in the trunk. Luckily, old Mercedes Benz sedans have trunks the size of Texas.

"Remain quiet," Ambrose says through the metal. "We just have to get through this gate and you're in." The car starts up and Ambrose pulls out.

"Don't even think about it," I say in the blackness.

"What?" Paulie whispers.

"You know what," I say, "letting one rip."

The three of us giggle as the Mercedes bounces down the bumpy road, but when the car slows, we become still. We hear a soldier say, "Good evening. May I see your clearance, please sir?"

We don't breathe. It seems like it's taking forever, then we hear the soldier say, "Ok, you're good to go." As the car pulls away, we exhale with a loud gush.

"I thought I might burst," Sara whispers.

"Shhhh," I say.

Ambrose drives for maybe five minutes and then the car stops. We hear him get out, come around, and open the trunk. I jump out. The night is so dark I can barely make out his frame. I suck in the fresh air and my tingly skin makes me feel alive.

We are parked near an electric fence surrounding an airfield. Ambrose puts his arm around my shoulders and points. "You see that Quonset hut bunker out there, about 200 meters from the edge of the airstrip?"

My eyes are adjusting to the darkness. I see a small structure with a couple of lights off in the distance. "Yes," I answer him.

"That's your target. One or two soldiers will be manning the bunker. Since the base closure, there is rarely activity, so they won't be expecting you. You need to get in and out without them noticing."

I step back and stare blankly at him. The small trunk light gives us a tiny bit of illumination. Sara and Paulie wait patiently, squatting in the trunk.

"Um, doc...how is that possible?" I ask. "They'll see us as

soon as we walk through the door. Speaking of that…how are we supposed to get in?"

"I will explain everything, Jake," Ambrose says. "Now, kids, get out." He motions to Paulie and Sara, then faces me, both hands on my shoulders. "I will be monitoring you the whole time. However, I will not be able to come to your rescue, understood?"

"Understood," I say. I huddle with Paulie and Sara. "Listen, guys, it's not too late to back out. You can stay here with Ambrose and wait for me."

"No way," Paulie says emphatically. "I didn't come all this way to wait in the car like a baby. I'm ready for some action."

I smile. Good old Paulie.

"What about you, Sara? It's not too late."

She shakes her head. "You're not getting rid of me now, Jake."

I put one arm around Sara's shoulders and the other around Paulie's. "Thanks, guys."

Ambrose grabs wire cutters and a black metal case from the trunk. At the fence, he opens the case and takes out something that looks like jumper cables: two cords of thick, plastic-coated wire. One end is attached to the equipment inside the case and the other is large alligator clips which Ambrose holds. "These will allow us to cut the fence without arousing suspicion by rerouting the electrical current through this metal box," he says. He hands me one of the cables. "Here, Jake. Attach this to the fence about waist high." Ambrose attaches the other alligator clip about three feet away from me. After making sure both clips are secured, Ambrose returns to the case and turns a knob, rerouting the electricity through the case so that we can chop a hole in the fence large enough for us to fit through. The fence cutters are industrial strength, sharp and strong; it takes less than a minute to get the job done.

We wait for Ambrose's direction. He puts his index finger to his lips in the universal sign of *Be Quiet* and then touches his finger to his ear. I realize he is listening through his comms device. "Uh, huh. Yes. Ok. We are ready," he says to someone at the lab. He motions the three of us together. "Jake, you remember what Miriam did with Gertrude?"

I nod.

"Well, the same is about to happen to you three. You will be able to see each other, but no one else will." Sara and Paulie stare bug-eyed at Ambrose, speechless.

"So, that's how we're getting in," I say, disbelieving.

Ambrose grins like a happy child. "Yes, Jake! Still, you must be very quiet…"

Paulie interrupts. "Like, stealth, right? Undercover brother!"

"Really?" I glare at Paulie, and then say to Ambrose, "Go on, doc."

"They will not be able to see you, but if you make a noise, they may hear you."

"Right. Got it," I say to Ambrose. "You two got it?"

Paulie and Sara nod in unison.

"So, are you ready to go?" Ambrose asks.

The three of us head for the opening in the fence, and then I stop, remembering something. "But, doc, how are we supposed to get into the bunker? They must have top end security."

"Oh, yes, yes…I nearly forgot." Ambrose jogs back to the trunk and motions me to follow. He grabs another small black container. "Here, Jake."

"Not another shot, please doc."

"No, Jake. I need your thumb and your eye, please."

"Huh?"

Ambrose chuckles as he reaches for my thumb and rolls it over a tiny screen. An imprint of my thumb appears. "Now, look at me, Jake," Ambrose says. "Don't blink." I stare at him and he runs a scanner across my right iris. "Now we have your thumb print and your iris scan," he says, closing the box. "Just in case."

"You certainly did come prepared, doc."

He pats me on the back. "Get going, Jake. And, remember, they are monitoring your every move back at the lab. When you reach the door, we will provide whatever tech is necessary to open it for you."

I pull my ski mask over my head. Paulie dons a Freddie Kruger Halloween job which he's painted over with black magic marker. Sara's mask is pink— I should have known— with white tufts of bunny tails. I stare in disbelief. "Is that the best you could do?" I ask, shaking my head. It's all a precaution, anyway, as we won't be visible. "Come on." I signal them to follow me through the hole in the fence.

CHAPTER 23
INSANE NINJA WARRIOR MISSION

Inside the fence we squat down and look around. All's quiet on the airstrip and in the field leading to the Quonset hut. I remind myself what Ambrose said at the car: back at the lab, they are seeing and hearing everything. It's a comforting thought.

"Wait!" Ambrose has that strange look on his face again, like he's listening. Then he speaks to the lab, "Yes, they are inside the perimeter. Proceed as planned."

"Jake," Ambrose calls out quietly. "Miriam will perform the de-materialization now."

"What!?" I whisper-yell back.

"I don't know if I like the sound of that," Paulie says.

Ambrose says each word slowly, in a hushed tone, "She... will...transmute...you."

Paulie and Sara gape at me.

"It's ok," I reassure them. "A woman named Miriam is going to make our energy field disappear to the naked eye, just like she did with a chimp in the lab."

A glazed pallor covers Paulie's face, like someone just told him he would never eat again.

"Snap out of it, dude," I say.

"Is *that* what you saw in the lab?" he asks me.

"Just one of the super-rad things I saw there, bro. You wouldn't believe it. It was frackin awesome!" I grin. I can tell he totally gets it.

"It's done," Ambrose calls to us in his whisper voice. He's staring past us. "I can no longer see you."

You would think, when your energy field gets messed with, you'd feel something, but I don't feel any different. I look at Paulie and Sara and they both appear normal to me. I bring my hands up to my face. I can see myself just fine. Ambrose is peering through the fence though, searching, as if we don't exist. "Are you there, Jake?"

"We're here, doc. No worries," I assure him.

"Yes, yes. Ok, good. I will get into my car and tune in through comms. Good luck!"

Sara and Paulie stare idly, as if they don't understand what all the fuss is about.

"We're invisible," I say, deadpan.

"Yeah, right," Sara says.

"Trust me." I confirm.

"Oh—kaaaaeeeyyy," Sara says, unconvinced.

"Frakkin awesome!" Paulie exclaims.

"Come on. No time to waste," I wave at them to follow me. "Keep your voices down. Remember, they can't see us, but they can hear us, okay?"

"Got it," Paulie says. "Let's rock this place."

"Let's just get in and out as unobtrusively as possible, please," I order them.

"Yes, sir, Jake sir," Paulie says, imitating a soldier.

I let this go as we make our way to the Quonset hut. I take a last look over my shoulder and suddenly I hear Ambrose inside my head, literally. "Don't worry, Jake." He's speaking through the microchip. "We are all here with you." It's a bizarre sensation, realizing that he and his assistants are experiencing everything through my eyes and ears.

I signal for Paulie and Sara to follow me across the open divide between the fence and the Quonset hut. I feel exhilarated—a brew of excited and terrified. I turn around to assure myself that the Mercedes is still parked by the fence. Suddenly, I hear a distinctive *FWAP-FWAP* sound coming from the airstrip. A helicopter has taken off and is flying in our direction, headlight beaming outward into the night. *We are dead, as vulnerable as pigeons with their wings clipped, out here in this open field.*

"RUN!" I yell, taking a risk that I won't be heard over the chopper. I don't know a lot about helicopters, but I can tell it's a formidable one, probably an Apache attack chopper or one of those stealth Black Hawks.

I'm not a runner, but I pump my legs like I'm trying to win a marathon. We're at least a hundred yards from the hut. I look back. Sara is, as always, directly behind me. Paulie is not. He's about twenty yards behind us. *He's never going to make it.*

"JAKE!" Ambrose yells in my head, waking me from this bad dream. "You're invisible!" he says.

I stop dead and put my hands on my knees, breathing hard. I don't think I've ever felt so stupid in my life. How could I forget? *Well, perhaps because you've never been invisible before?* I comfort myself.

Sara bumps into me, knocking me over. I rest my head on

my knees, my butt on the cold ground. It's difficult to hear over the noise of the chopper as it navigates towards us. Its massive headlight maneuvers back and forth across a wide swath of the field, eventually lighting up Paulie. I gulp. The dirt beneath us stirs. The ominous, black devil is directly above us, so close that we cover our eyes to protect from debris. Just when I'm sure we must be discovered, the chopper continues on—leaving us like almost-squashed bugs, to live another day. The metallic *fwap* of the chopper blades fade away as the aircraft moves off to the west.

Paulie lumbers up and whispers the obvious. "Why were you guys freaking out? I thought we were supposed to be invisible," he says, hands on hips. "Speaking of that..." He pulls the ridiculous Freddie Kruger mask off his face.

I shake my head. "Okay, okay. You got me. I spaced it."

They both put out a hand to help me up. Now we really are a team.

"Everybody all right?" Ambrose asks.

"Yeah, we're fine, doc," I answer.

Paulie, Sara and I continue towards the dimly lit Quonset hut. A jeep is parked outside. We circle the hut several times, but we can't find a door, or anything that looks like an entrance.

"Doc?" I whisper.

"Yes, Jake. I'm here," Ambrose answers in my head. "Circumnavigate the building again, please."

I signal Paulie and Sara to stay put while I perform another go-around.

"Ah, there it is," Ambrose says.

"What?" I ask him.

"You see that plant near the corner, the one that looks like a small palm tree?

"Yes."

"I believe that is a camouflaged entrance," he says. "Pull the fronds aside, please."

I gently move the palm fronds to one side, and sure enough, I see a coded security box at chest level, although nothing around it looks like a door.

"Aha!" Ambrose exclaims. "Now, let's get you in." I'm suddenly aware of how strange it would appear if someone saw me talking to this plant.

Ambrose makes me focus. "Please open the box and look inside, Jake."

I do as I'm told. The box contains a keypad, a small screen, and a red button.

"It's a good thing we took that iris scan, Jake," Ambrose says. "This entry requires a secret code *and* an iris scan. Give the lab a moment to decipher the code."

"Ok, doc. I'm gonna go get Paulie and Sara."

"Quickly, Jake," he responds.

Paulie and Sara are scrunched down together back-to-back, like a couple of soldiers on the front line.

"You're invisible, remember?" I whisper, smirking. "Come on. We found a way in."

Back at the entry box, Ambrose says, "Ok, Jake, we have narrowed the possibilities for the code to one hundred and twelve."

"Oh, only one hundred and twelve, huh?" I ask, incredulously.

"That ought to take a few hours," Paulie whispers. "Maybe I'll use this opportunity to catch up on my sleep."

"Pipe down. The less patter, the better," I tell him. Paulie shrugs and leans on the metal hut. A hook from his small backpack clangs against it.

"Whadja bring that for?" I ask, expecting to get caught any moment.

"Don't get mad," he says. "I brought energy bars. I didn't know when we'd eat again. Plus, there might be some cool stuff in there."

"This isn't a trip to the mall, Paulie!" It's hard not to yell.

"Sorry." Paulie looks genuinely chastised.

Sara pulls Paulie off the wall of the hut. "It's ok, Jake. Just do what you have to do."

"Jake?" Ambrose questions in my head.

"Yeah, yeah…I'm here…just dealing with some employee infractions."

"We must stay focused, Jake. Now, please stand in front of the box again."

I do as I'm told.

"We are going to narrow this down very rapidly, okay?"

"Whatever you say, doc," I answer, careful to speak softly.

"Please enter the following numbers on the keypad: 2-7-9-5-4."

I enter the numbers. Nothing happens.

"Ok, now enter them backwards."

I enter: 4-5-9-7-2. Nothing happens.

"It's ok, Jake. We are sequencing all the possibilities for this particular model. It will only take a minute."

At this point, I would believe anything Ambrose might tell me. Why not? After what I've witnessed today, I'm like the kid who meets an alien for the first time. I'm a believer.

I'm startled by a new voice, someone from the lab. "Try this one, Jake."

"Okay," I reply.

Reonne Haslett   **/**   171

"7-9-2-4-5...in that order, please."

I do as I'm told again. This time there is a perceptible *click*, but the door doesn't open.

"I think we've got it, folks," the lab assistant says in my head.

"Now, Jake, eyes on that screen, please," Ambrose commands me. "We are going to reprogram it with the scan we took of your iris. Give us a moment."

I can only imagine what's going on back at the lab to make all of this happen and I feel incredibly grateful. After a minute or two, Ambrose continues, "Ok, we're ready to go. Put your right eyeball up to that screen and when I say NOW, press the red button."

I do as he says. A fluorescent green line on the screen swishes back and forth across my vision. "Now!" Ambrose says, and I push the red button. Immediately a door-size section of the wall opens into an outer room, quiet and empty.

I signal Sara and Paulie to keep a look-out—my index and middle fingers point to the ground, then to my eyes.

Ambrose says, "Jake, I don't know what's in there, but I would look for a locked door or a vault, something like that. Believe it or not, the ENERGENX PROJECT code is probably just sitting in a file somewhere. It's a very old project and everybody has forgotten about it by now. Well, almost everybody..." he trails off.

"Got it, doc. Thanks for everything."

"I'll be seeing you soon, Jake, don't worry."

We sneak into the bunker like a trio of Ninja warriors, no idea what's in here, but ready for whatever it is.

CHAPTER 24
A THIEF AND TWO PRANKSTERS

Ambrose was right; two soldiers sit at computer consoles inside the hut, their backs to us. I put my index finger up to my ski mask-covered mouth and then point to Sara and Paulie's shoes. They get the message. We must move with extreme care, as stealth as a cat waiting at a gopher hole. Luckily for us, both soldiers are staring at monitors, wearing headphones, which may explain why they haven't heard our shenanigans so far. Both sport military crew cuts; the smaller soldier, dark-haired, the larger one, carrot-topped.

We three stand perfectly still. Those hours of crime thrillers are finally paying off—I seem to have downloaded the hand signals of a swat team leader. I keep my right palm face down to the ground signaling Paulie and Sara to hold still as I scan the room. Suddenly, Ambrose speaks and I'm sure everyone must have heard him, but no one moves.

"Look to your left…over there," Ambrose says. "Can you see that area that looks like a cage?" He quickly adds, "Don't answer, Jake."

In truth, I have to catch myself. I remind myself the lab can see and hear everything. I don't need to talk. Ambrose continues. "There's a good chance you will find the code in there."

Signaling to Sara and Paulie to keep still, I slowly and *very* carefully walk over to the cage. At the cage door I see the padlock is hanging, unclasped, and Ambrose says, "What good fortune, Jake!" I'm bolstered, knowing I'm not alone.

Sara and Paulie move forward into the room. The soldiers remain focused on their computer monitors. One of them laughs out loud, startling us. I put my palm face down again, signaling Sara and Paulie to remain motionless. I'm beginning to wonder if I was right to have dragged them along on this dangerous mission.

The dark-haired soldier shifts, his chair making a loud squeak, and Sara accidentally backs into a floor lamp, which causes it to flicker. She reaches out to steady it, but the red-headed guy notices the flicker and swings around. Sara stabilizes the lamp, and the soldier turns back to his screen. I can tell from across the room that Sara's nerves are unraveling, so I sign language to her with my fingers: I-T-S-O-K.

Once things have settled, I slowly push open the chain link gate to the file room. I put my hand over the jangling lock and inch the door wider, making sure I don't attract attention. I slip into the cage. I chance leaving the door open for ease of escape, as the soldiers haven't noticed anything thus far. Sara and Paulie remain glued to their shoes in the opposite corner, focused on me.

I spy an ancient metal four-drawer filing cabinet among the newer ones. The ENERGENX PROJECT file must be in there. The peeling labels on the outside of the drawers identify that the contents are in alphabetical order. The ENERGENX

PROJECT file should be in the first drawer labeled A–F. How am I going to get it open without making a sound? I put my thumb on the metal button and my fingers through the handle. When I push the button to the right, there is an audible *click*. I stop, wait. No movement from the soldiers. I'm suddenly grateful for headphones and the distractions of the internet.

Carefully, I pull the drawer out. It's quiet for such a dinosaur. I quickly search the folders but find nothing related to the ENERGENX PROJECT. *Oh, no!* I move to the second file drawer—a small clicking sound, and then the drawer slides noiselessly. They must keep them lubricated. Nothing in here either.

I hear Ambrose in my head. "Perhaps it's filed under TOP SECRET, Jake."

On the third drawer, there is no click...the button must be broken. Confidently, I pull the drawer out—the other two released so easily—but the drawer is half-way out and *SCREECH!* I feel my heart in my throat. Both soldiers look towards the cage. They see the door is open. They see a filing cabinet drawer open.

"What the....?" The redhead says as he pulls off his earphones and swivels his chair.

The dark-haired soldier takes off his headphones and stands at the ready. I'm beginning to panic. Should I close the drawer? Leave it open? Run out the door? The redhead is out of his chair and walking toward the cage. Suddenly, a coffee cup flies across the room. It lands right in front of him, splashing him with the dark brown liquid.

"What the...?" The redhead says again as he stares down at his coffee-stained clothes.

The dark-haired soldier leaps to help his buddy. Both soldiers seem confused, not knowing which way to turn—towards the cage, or the source of the tossed cup. And then, Sara and Paulie begin throwing everything they can get their hands on. Pens, pencils, paper clips, staplers, coffee cups, soar across the room.

The distraction works. The soldiers stomp in the direction the items are launching from. I seize the opportunity to search through the open file drawer but find nothing. My heart races and sweat drips into my eyes. I yank off the hot ski mask. I've got one more chance. I coax drawer number four open. I guess the fates are on my side because it slides easily.

Sara and Paulie continue their assault on the men, darting around the room, throwing various items, avoiding capture. It would be comical if I weren't scared out of my mind.

"Remember to breathe, Jake," I hear Ambrose's voice. "Focus."

Just hearing his calming voice helps me block out the antics in the room and search this last drawer. As I reach the back, I'm losing hope, and then I see it: TOP SECRET: ENERGENX PROJECT. I grab the folder. An old floppy disk falls out and slips underneath the filing cabinet. The red-headed soldier looks in my direction. "Hey," he says to his buddy and points. I realize what he's witnessing: a file folder flopping around in the air and the disk falling underneath the cabinet. I drop onto my stomach and frantically fish for it, but it is beyond my reach.

"It's okay, Jake," Ambrose says in my head. "Get out of there!"

"Let's go!" I blurt out. Like velociraptors sensing prey, the soldier's heads snap in the direction of my voice. Just then, Paulie hits the light switch, darkening the room. A visible glow emanates from the computer monitors and other electrical equipment, but it is much more difficult to see.

"Over there!" The redhead points and starts toward the cage. Before he gets far, Paulie trips him, and he topples to the floor. I'm out of the cage in two giant strides. Sara picks the coffee cup up off the floor and throws it at the dark-haired soldier. It hits him full force on the chest, knocking him off-balance. He back-steps, his feet stumbling over one another, then falls backward, his butt stuck inside a metal garbage can. He pushes on the sides, growling several expletives, but can't extricate himself. The can bounces up and down.

"Go! Go!" Ambrose says. I dive over the red-headed soldier, sprawled on the floor. He lunges for the file folder and takes a hold of it.

"No!" I scream. I grasp the folder and tug back.

"Give it to me," the redhead yells.

"Don't let him get out of here with that file," says the dark-haired man, struggling to free his butt from the can.

The redhead and I are in a tug of war with the file folder, and then, another coffee cup flies across the room. I've decided Sara should be entered into the coffee-cup-throwing hall of fame. It hits the redhead on the shoulder, just enough to make him slip sideways, giving me an advantage. As his grip loosens, I wrench hard. A few of the pages begin to slip out as we tussle. Finally, I win the battle and the file folder flies at me, but not without consequences—I hear a ripping sound as I gain control. There's no time to stop now, but I notice a shred of paper in the soldier's hand as he struggles to get up. While we were fighting over the folder, Paulie snuck in and tied an extension cord around his ankles.

"Come on!" I yell at Sara and Paulie. The dark-haired soldier is pushing with all his might on the rim of the trash can, his legs flailing; the red-headed soldier is flopping around like a fish out of water, trying to untie the cord from his ankles. "Sorry, guys," I say to them as we dash out the door.

Sara, Paulie and I sprint like our lives depend on it. Our invisibility must be dissolving as we reach the fence because Ambrose reaches directly for Sara and pulls her through the hole. I push Paulie through and then Ambrose has got me by the shoulders. He shakes me. "Good work, Jake!" he says. "Now let's get out of here."

I'm certain that, at any moment, sirens will wail, and spotlights will illuminate us. But nothing remotely like that happens. Did the soldiers extricate themselves by now? Will they alert the guards at the gate? My mind and heart are racing. Will they clean up the Quonset hut and keep this evening's events to themselves? What's one little ancient file folder when their careers are at risk? They still have the floppy disk after all. Would they want anybody to know that three invisible kids got the better of them? I'm hoping not.

We remove the alligator clips from the fence and climb into Ambrose's trunk. The three of us are silent as we drive back toward the gate. I realize I'm holding my breath, waiting for the worst to happen, but we hear nothing; no sirens or loudspeakers ordering us to pull over. The Mercedes exits the gate as smoothly as it entered.

After we leave the base, Ambrose pulls over in the military housing neighborhood. He lets us out of the trunk, and we climb into the backseat, leaning on each other for comfort. The sky remains dark and serene, stars twinkling, on the drive back to the lab. I stare at the file I'm holding tightly in my lap. I can't stop thinking, "We got away with it! I've got the ENERGENX PROJECT file!" I take a mini flashlight out of my pocket and hold it between my teeth as I peruse the pages, searching for the one with the code. *Wait, there's a problem.* I frantically ruffle through the pages. "NO!" I scream. "It can't be!"

Ambrose immediately pulls the car over to the side of the road. He turns around in his seat. "What is it, Jake?" I hold up a torn page, the one the soldier ripped right before we ran out the door. Sara takes the page from me and hands it to Ambrose. He turns the overhead light on.

"What? What is it?" Paulie asks.

"I'm so sorry, Jake," Ambrose says.

"For God's sake…what?" Paulie implores us.

I look at Paulie, trying to hold back the tears welling up in my eyes. I can't speak. Ambrose jumps in for me. "It's the code, Paulie. Part of it is missing."

CHAPTER 25
A LESSON IN MORPHING

can barely hold my head up. My body aches and my heart
feels shattered. My throat feels like I've been gargling sand.
I can't speak.

Upon entering the base, I was excited and determined, but
now, any hope I had of finding Oshi is dashed. She feels a
million miles away, out of reach.

Sara puts her hand on my shoulder. "Jake, it's going to be
all right. We'll figure something out."

Paulie chimes in with his usual positivity. "Yeah, Jake. No
worries, bro. We'll find her. You'll see."

Ambrose pulls the black Mercedes into the well-lit parking
lot behind the lab, its shadow spreading across the asphalt.
Even though I feel paralyzed with exhaustion and anger, I drag
myself out of the car. My shadow merges with the Mercedes',
as dark as I feel.

Ambrose speaks through his earpiece to someone in the
lab. "We are back. Open the door and brew me some strong
coffee...and make the kids some cocoa."

Several white-coated lab assistants emerge from the
building. They usher us in with congratulatory pats on the

back. I'm numb to their kudos. We walk past the chimps who acknowledge us with hoots and hollers. My brain is fried. I don't have an ounce of energy left to piece together what needs to happen next.

And then, I hear a familiar voice, "Jake."

I look up, and there stands my father.

"Dad?" He catches me in his arms. "I failed," I lament. "I tried everything. Now she's lost forever."

"You're very brave," Dad whispers.

Sara slams into us. "Dad!"

"I'm glad you kids are safe. Your mom's worried sick."

"I was afraid of that," Sara says as she takes a step back.

Dad lets go of me. "Jake, Ambrose explained everything to me, but I'm not sure I approve of your tactics, especially dragging your little sister and your friend here into it."

Paulie looks sheepishly at my father. "It's okay, Mr. Green, really."

"How did you find out, Dad?" I ask him.

He offers me a chair. Sara stands next to me. "Your mom called me as soon as she saw the note," he says.

"Yeah, but...how did you know where to find me?"

Dad and Ambrose exchange looks. "Ambrose called me," Dad says.

"But...how did Ambrose...?" They watch intently as I connect the dots. A small smile forms on Ambrose's lips. Suddenly, it dawns on me. "No. Way!" I face my father. "You're the 'Dr. J', aren't you? On the document!" Dad cups his hands behind his back and shuffles his feet. He nods.

"Dr. Ambrose Lavinski, Dr. Buckminster Stone and Dr. Justin Green," I say, amazed.

He nods again.

"Enough of these sentimentalities," Ambrose says, as he puts his arm around my shoulders and directs me to the pod. We stare up at it. "We must get you into that website."

"Huh? But I don't have the code. It's in between the fingers of some soldier with his ankles tied together." I hand the page to my father.

"What happened, Jake?" he asks me.

"It's a long story, Dad, but there was a fight over the ENERGENX PROJECT file, and when I finally got control of it, a page ripped. I didn't know it was the page with the code until we were back in the car."

"I see," is all he says. He paces, staring at the paper, rubbing his chin, then turns to Ambrose and asks, "May I use your office for a moment?"

"Certainly," Ambrose answers and then commands his assistants. "Prep the pod!"

The assistants scurry, readying equipment and checking instruments. I follow my dad into Ambrose's office. My heart tells me what he's going to do, but my mind can't grasp it.

"Dad? Are you gonna…"

He waves a hand at me, picks up an eraser and clears the Plexiglas board. Fixedly, he studies the torn page. He picks up a black Expo marker and writes on the board, code streaming from his fingers like a maestro conducting an orchestra. He scribbles like a man possessed, erasing numbers with his palm, and rewriting new ones. Several minutes pass. I stare in awe as the board fills. Suddenly, he stops, takes a deep breath, and sits down.

"Dad? Are you okay?" I ask.

"Glass of water, Jake...please," he says, his voice a bit ragged. "Although, I'd prefer something stronger." Dad glances up at me from under his brow, searching my face for a reaction. "It calms my nerves, helps me focus." When I don't respond he adds, "But not tonight, right? We're on a mission."

I set the water in front of him. He empties the glass in two gulps then rests his forehead in his hands, elbows on the desk, staying that way for a long time. I don't know whether he's recollecting the past or gone off to la-la land. Will his calibrating mind be able to piece together the code? I stand there, numb, not knowing what to do, as the clock ticks. I don't dare disturb him. Suddenly, he jumps up.

"That's it!" he exclaims, and frantically scrawls on the board. He speaks in short bursts. "I wasn't sure...I could remember... Jake. I thought...I was going to...let you down. But it came back to me. Just...like...that." These last words he emphasizes as he strokes the last three numbers of the code. "And I did it without the booze," he says happily. "Come on, Jake. Help me!" He wheels the Plexiglas board toward Ambrose's office door. "Open it. Open it."

I open the door, and together we maneuver the board over to the pod.

"This is it, Ambrose!" my dad says, tapping the board a bit too forcefully with the marker.

"You did it, Justin! Fine work. I couldn't remember the code if my life depended on it." Ambrose applauds my dad, then says to his assistants, "Let's get Jake suited up."

I begin to sweat as a tight knot forms in my stomach. I'm petrified. Everything up until now has been fascinating and illuminating, but at least it's been in this paradigm. Now I'm about to enter the World Wide Web. I can't wrap my mind around it.

"Don't be afraid, Jake," says Ambrose. "We will be with you all the way. Remember the chip? We'll bring you back immediately if there are any problems, any problems at all, ok?"

I fix my lips and nod, but my guts are churning. A lab assistant thrusts a white spacesuit and a bulky helmet at me. "Here." The spacesuit is made of lightweight material, but the helmet is heavy. "NASA created this," she says. "Put it on over your clothes."

Sara's slouched in a chair, an expression of amazement on her face. Paulie jaunts around the lab chatting with lab workers, and, not surprisingly, feeding the chimps bits of his energy bar.

In the bathroom I realize how long it's been since I've taken a pee. I stand there, looking in the mirror, face to face with myself. Like Sara said this morning, I look haggard, for sure, but also older. I've been through a lot in the past few days, and it shows. I finish my business, wash my hands, and splash cold water on my face. It's refreshing. I smooth my hair with my wet hands. "Well, this is it," I say out loud to my reverse image. "The moment you've been working towards. Go and find your best friend."

If someone had told me three days ago that I would be strapped into an experimental pod in the Paranormal Research Department at Stanford University, about to be injected into the World Wide Web, I would have laughed my ass off and asked them what kind of drugs they were on. But here I am.

An assistant helps me climb into the pod. Ambrose runs around, barking orders. He stops and peers up at me. "Everything ok in there, Jake? Are you comfortable?" His voice sounds far away and muffled.

I can't take my eyes off my father, hunkered down at the control panel, looking very serious. *Well, it is most definitely serious, isn't it?* I force my attention on Ambrose. "I'm fine, doc." Then I stare at my dad again. His only son is about to disappear before his eyes, using technology he helped create. He witnessed two human beings transported into the web, never to return. Dad and Ambrose may have been more fearless back then, willing to try anything, but the government put the kibosh on the project after the test subjects were never seen again. "Lost in the line of duty" was the official statement.

But this time is different, right? Ambrose developed this new pod himself, improving upon the original design, plus, we have twenty-five years of advanced technology on our side. I'm going to go in there, find Oshi, and get out quickly. *At least, that's what I'm telling myself.*

A loud rumbling noise startles me, then a whirring sound emanates from below. My eyes feel like they're bulging out from their sockets. Ambrose's lips form a reassuring smile, the wrinkles around his eyes crinkling. "Don't worry, Jake," he says. "We're just starting up the pod."

I force a smile, but I'm not sure he can see my expression, so I bob the heavy helmet back and forth on my neck. The lab has been cleared of all nonessential personnel. Only Ambrose's most trusted assistants remain to facilitate the unauthorized experiment. I know Ambrose is putting himself on the line for me, and the fact that I'm Justin's son...if anything should happen to me...but I don't let myself think about *that.*

My dad looks up at me from the controls and mouths, "I... love...you."

"I love you too, Dad," I respond. My sentiment is heard

throughout the lab. My microchip is now hooked-up to the network again.

"Are we ready to go?" Ambrose calls to my dad, who nods his assent. Ambrose is in my head. "You might feel a little something. I'm not sure what because we...."

"I know, doc." I interrupt him. "You were never able to interview the other two guys."

Ambrose takes his glasses off and cleans them vigorously on his lab coat. "This technology has been significantly improved since then, Jake. Even though we were never able to run tests, I have the highest confidence in it. And remember, we will be with you all the way." He positions his glasses back on his head.

I'm extremely aware of my jitters. It's claustrophobic in the pod. I take a couple of deep breaths. I can see Sara and Paulie off in the background. They both wave and Paulie gives me a thumbs up. I can't raise my arm to reply, so I just nod my helmet as big as I can. It clunks against the back and front of the pod.

A thunderous growl shakes me. I feel like I'm about to rocket to the moon, but I know the pod itself won't be going anywhere, just me. I hear a voice over by the control panel, "All systems go, Dr. Lavinski," and I brace myself for...well... whatever might happen. Ambrose gives me a double thumbs up, and in seconds, I'm morphing! My body tingles and it feels like I'm being zapped with electrical pulses from my feet to my head and back down again. The accompanying sound is like a vibrating *WHA, WHA, WHA.*

Hundreds of distinct circles orbit my body, circular lines of varying colors with every hue on the planet, from violet to gold, turquoise to crimson, emerald to coral. The colorful orbit moves faster and faster until it is a blur, until I am a blur.

I'm on fire from the inside out.

I knew I should have been worried when Ambrose said, *you might feel a little something*. Like, *this might hurt a bit*, when he jammed the microchip into my head. *Yeah, right, Ambrose*. This feels like I'm about to explode into a million tiny particles. I'll be a pool of goo in the bottom of the pod if something doesn't happen soon.

I can't make out anything in the lab. All I see are thousands of tiny, spinning specs. And there is pain—pain in my head, my back, my arms, my legs. I want to scream for someone to let me out, when, suddenly, there is nothingness.

CHAPTER 26
INSIDE GOTCHU

When I come to, I'm aware only of the sound of my breath, in...out...in...out. Afraid to move, I remain still, eyes closed. My neck's bent at an awkward angle inside the helmet. I slowly roll onto my back and remove it. I take a short breath to test the air and don't keel over.

The floor feels cold beneath me and the first thing I'm aware of is the silence—the most silent silence I've ever experienced. Not like library silence, where you can hear a pin drop, or movie theatre silence, where you chomp your popcorn while you wait with anticipation, or doctor's office silence, where magazine pages flip and everybody seems nervous. This is more like the *absence of sound*, like what I imagine it might be like to be deaf.

I'm afraid to look, afraid to know where I am. *Did this really happen?* I muster the courage and lift my eyelids. What the absence of sound is to my ears, the absence of sight is to my eyes. It is nothingness—no objects, textures, or colors—only a palling grayness.

Even though I feel disoriented, I force myself to sit up. Everywhere I look is sameness. It's impossible to get my

187

bearings. I set the helmet down and slowly stand. I reach out a helpless hand. If I were to explore, I wouldn't know which way to go. Is this where those two guys from the first experiment ended up? Walking endlessly through this void until they died of thirst and starvation?

Get a hold of yourself, Jake. I'm not alone. I'm not alone, I'm not alone. I repeat this mantra, hands fisted at my sides. Suddenly, I remember the chip in my head.

I'm afraid to break the deep quiescence of this place, so I speak in the softest whisper I can manage, "Doc?"

He's with me in an instant. "Dzięki Bogu! Jake, I'm here." His voice sounds so loud in my head it makes me shudder.

"There's no sound here, Doc," I barely whisper. "Can you talk a little softer, please?"

"Sure, Jake. What are you experiencing? Describe your surroundings."

"Uh...I can try," I offer. "Let's see. Rather than there being something to describe, I would have to say there's an absence of anything to describe. It's as if I've been transported into nothingness."

"Hmmm...yes, we see that here as well," he confirms.

"How do I get into the Gotchu site?" I ask.

"Let me confer with the group and I'll get right back to you," he answers.

Ambrose is gone and I realize I'm trembling. I can feel my heart pounding in my chest. But I also feel a sense of urgency. I need to check this place out, get going. I decide it's best to do this in circles, so I don't get too far from where I woke up. I need something to orient me, to keep track of my starting point. I remember the pack of gum in my jeans pocket and get an idea.

I unzip the front of my spacesuit, wriggle out of it, and grab the gum. While I chew a piece, I step out about two feet from where I left the spacesuit and walk around it. Nothing happens. I stick the gum to the floor where I'm standing. I walk out five more feet, circle around and still nothing happens. I stick another piece of chewed gum to the floor. I continue to do this until I'm about twenty feet out from the original gob of gum. No matter how far I go, everything remains silent and gray. It's disappointing, plus now there's gum all over the floor.

"Jake?" Ambrose says in my head.

"Here, doc."

"We've deliberated and have come to the conclusion that now is the time for you to try your psychokinetic skills."

"My *what?*"

"Remember what we talked about in the lab? About how most people use less than 10 percent of their brains?"

"Yeah, I remember."

Ambrose continues, "Well, I'm going to ask you to sit down, close your eyes, and concentrate. Your dad is decoding data for the Gotchu site right now. Hang on…" Ambrose goes offline for a moment. I decide to sit right where I am. He comes back on. "We're going to send some code to the chip, Jake. If this goes how we hope, you should be able to see it forming as a picture in your head."

I close my eyes and focus. I'm aware of a flicker of light, like a fluorescent yellow flash in my head.

"We're sending it now, Jake. Are you getting anything?"

"I am! I am!" I say, startled, as I see bright yellow code glowing on a black screen. "I can see the code. It's in my head…

or wait...it's on the back of my eyelids. I don't know. It's hard to explain, doc, but I see it."

"Good, good," he says. "Now, we have a strong sense that if you concentrate on this code, you will be able to transport yourself into the site. You must be totally focused though, Jake, and not let any other thoughts enter your mind. Miriam is here too, and she is going to focus on the code with you. Please begin."

I summon any pictures I've ever seen of meditation—gurus, yogis, and such—and sit with my legs crossed placing my hands on my knees. With my eyes closed, I focus intently on the code in my head.

Ambrose speaks softly, "Jake? Miriam suggests that you breathe in through your nose and out through your mouth very slowly. She says this will aid the process."

I breathe—in, out, in, out. Nothing happens.

"I'm a failure at this woo-woo stuff, doc," I say.

"Continue to breathe, Jake," Ambrose says. "In through the nose, out through the mouth. Eyes closed. Focus on the code. Focus on the code." His tone is hypnotic, lulling me deeper into a meditative state.

My mind begins to wander. Before I know it, I'm thinking about computer gear and Oshi and school and anything *but* the code. *STOP*, I tell myself. *Get back to breathing and focusing.* This mind battle continues for several minutes. I'm about to give up, and then, I feel a *WHOOSH* and sounds fill my ears. They startle me awake. I open my eyes and I'm sitting in the intersection near the Chinese laundry.

No. Way! It's as lifelike as when Paulie, Sara and I were running from Scarface. But wait—it's different. Something is

OFF here. The streetlights blink from red to yellow and then back to red. There's no green. It's like a ghost town, no people. There's no climate either—no breeze, no sun, no heat, no cold. The noises I hear are disconcerting. It's a loop of the same sounds over and over; a cat meows, birds chirp, a train whistle off in the distance. Then the *beep-blurp, beep-blurp* sound of the crosswalk which lets people know it's okay to walk, but the words on the crossing screen say DO NOT WALK. I can hear engines rumbling, brakes squealing and horns honking, but there are no cars. And then the sound loop plays all over again: cat, birds, train, *beep-blurp*, cars. Programmed, of course. All of this is programming.

"Doc?"

I'm surprised when my dad answers. "Hi Jake. We're here."

"I'm in. Now to find Oshi."

"Let us know if we can help."

"Just knowing you are there is helping me. Thanks, Dad, for everything."

"Of course, son."

I decide to check out the cleaners and Joe's place. The entrance to the building looks the same, but when I open the glass door I'm startled by white blankness, like a blizzard without the cold, snow, and wind. They only programmed the street and the facades, not what's inside the buildings. Okay, I can go with this. I design games. I understand how this works. The only difference is that I'm inside the game now, and it's a game of life or death.

I stand on the sidewalk and rub my head. What do I do next? How do I find Oshi? Should I yell for her? Stroll the street until I run into more white-out? Maybe I should have had a plan, but then, how could I have planned for *THIS?* It feels so crazy I want to laugh out loud.

I decide to sit down on the curb and reorient myself to being inside the website, inside this new paradigm. This is the intersection where I first saw Oshi in the video, but she's not here. If I can transport myself into this virtual world, maybe I can transport myself around the site. Maybe Oshi is at the location of the second video, the empty swimming pool. I close my eyes and concentrate. Code glimmers in my head.

When I open my eyes, I'm in the backyard with the empty pool. *I did it!* Just like the intersection, it's deserted and has an artificial feeling. The sound loop here is a dog barking, kids splashing, lawnmower, and then the same cat meow and bird chirps as the other loop. I don't remember hearing these sounds in the video. I was so focused on trying to figure out what Oshi was saying, I didn't notice. It's likely they hadn't been programmed yet. I don't really care. All I know is that Oshi isn't here either.

The back gate of the fence opens onto an alley that borders several backyards. I step out and notice unfamiliar architecture—pointed steeples, gables, grand porches, brick walls and gingerbread trim—probably designed by a New York or London programmer.

The end of the alley meets another street. I look right and left and all I see is blinding white-out. What a lame site. These guys could have used a little more imagination, but then, I have no idea what Gotchu is supposed to be...a social networking site? A game? A front for some other covert operation?

It feels eerie, like being on the set of a big budget movie when the cast and crew have gone to lunch. I turn around and start back toward the pool. As I get closer to the backyard, I hear the sound loop again: dog barking, water splashing, mower, cat, birds. *But wait…what's that? Do I hear voices?*

I tiptoe quietly and peek through the fence. Teenagers are hanging out by the pool. I recognize some of them from the videos. They shove each other, snorting and giggling. Something seems unnatural about them. I push my nose between fence slats to get a better look. One guy punches another on the shoulder, but his fist sinks in, like he's hitting the Pillsbury Dough Boy. Still, no Oshi.

"Jake?" Ambrose says in my head. Startled, I scratch my nose on the fence. I can't answer him right now, lest I draw attention to myself, so I tiptoe back up the alley.

"Doc," I whisper. "I have to be careful. You can see I've found some kids. I don't want them to hear me." But it's too late. When I look back down the alley, twelve teenagers with attitude are marching straight towards me, and I've got nowhere to go.

CHAPTER 27

FINALLY—OSHI

The Gotchu teenagers have stopped six feet in front of me. Up close there is something conspicuously off-kilter about them, over-the-top. One tall guy has pink and black striped hair combed straight up into a giant mohawk. He's dressed in skin-tight black leggings, black boots, and a black pleather jacket with chains. He's leaning on the shoulder of a shorter guy with neon orange hair, and baggy jeans that hang so low his plaid boxer shorts are all that's covering his butt. A girl with so much black eyeliner you can barely see her eyeballs, scrolls on an oversized smartphone. Another girl wears silver-sequined pants and spiked heels that would make a fashion model topple over. She holds hands with a girl wearing oversized square sunglasses and a faux fur mini-skirt, boots, and hat.

One kid holds a skateboard painted with outlandish graffiti. His long, straight, blonde hair, hangs to his waist. The funniest one is a comic book character of a rapper—baggy clothes, gold chains and floppy tennis shoes. A giant red and white striped hat, ala' The Cat and The Hat, teeter-totters on his head. Mixed with these are several other comical caricatures of teenage culture. They chew gum with loud, smacking motions and smoke cigarettes with huge puffs, exhaling "O's". Their laughter is forced and loud, and they strike each other with great fanfare, as if it's nothing out of the ordinary for teenagers to be constantly pushing, shoving, and poking each other.

The more peculiar thing is, when they do invade each other's space, it's as if they meld into one another. No one seems to get hurt and their movements are fluid. I also get the distinct impression that they are of one mind, as if a puppet master is pulling their strings.

"Where's Oshi?" I demand.

Instead of answering, they regard one another, then burst out laughing and elbow and jab each other again. *This is getting old.*

I try again. "Look, I know you've got my friend in here somewhere. Where is she?"

They move as a unit toward me. It's so sudden, they throw me off guard and I stumble backwards. More gum smacking, smoking, laughter, poking, pushing, and punching. Finally, the tall one with the pink and black mohawk speaks up. "We don't know any *Oshi.*" Loud guffaws emit from his cohorts. The girls giggle and cackle way longer than normal. I feel like I'm dealing with demons.

"I saw her here," I say with conviction.

The sequined-pants girl and the fur-skirted girl speak in unison, "Sooooo?"

"She doesn't want to be here. She wants to go back to the real world," I tell them.

The gang looks stymied. The orange-haired guy with the baggy pants says, "Home? Real World? What the hell you talkin about, bruh?"

I remind myself that these are avatars, unconscious creatures existing in this fake world. Creative programmers gave birth to this dirty dozen, which makes them even more dangerous. It's going to take wits and cunning to deal with them. I feel the need to check in with the lab.

"Doc?" I whisper, remaining perfectly still.

The programmed posse stands poised, waiting to react to my next move.

"Yes, Jake," he answers.

"Are you getting this?"

"Yes, we are. What do you make of it?"

"One thing's for certain, these aren't human. These are avatars—a personalized graphic controlled by its programmer. I'm just not sure how much they're coded to do. They seem so humanoid."

"Hmmm..." Ambrose responds. "What do you propose, Jake?"

"Not quite sure yet, doc, I..."

And then, just as quickly as they came up the alley, the Gotchu gang turns around and marches back toward the house with the pool. I wait until they disappear inside the gate, then creep slowly down the alley to observe. Their pseudo teenage behavior is embarrassing. *I mean, who programmed these kids? Boomers?* Teenagers aren't this ridiculous. Then I hear it, resounding off all the simulated buildings, streets, fences, and trash cans—Oshi's voice.

"JAKE! JAKE!"

My guts go cold. The Gotchu gang stops and listens too. They cock their heads, like a pack of zombies, ready to attack. Pink hair, skateboard dude, sequined-pants, fur skirt, rapper, all of them, run towards the gate. Not knowing which way to turn I race down the alley in the opposite direction.

"OSHI! Where are you?" I call out.

"I hear you Jake," Oshi yells. "Near a dry cleaner?"

At the end of the alley, another street, white-out in both directions. The avatars are almost upon me. I need the fastest way back to the intersection. I take a chance and turn right, into the blinding whiteness. I close my eyes and code my way back to the intersection. Instantly, I'm sitting on the curb in front of the Chinese laundry. And there, in the middle of the intersection, is Oshi, looking disheveled and confused.

She runs toward me and then, *PING, PANG, POONG...* the Gotchu gang materializes one by one between us, forming a line across the intersection. Their exaggerated antics continue, but seem more restrained, yet somehow more deadly, which can only mean their coders are standing at-the-ready to wipe us out.

"We're getting out of here and you're not going to stop us," I bellow out.

Oshi yells, "They're psychos, Jake! Get out of my way!" she screams at them.

Suddenly, I get an idea. I was able to stop Stone's virus from attacking millions of computers, maybe I can delete these avatars with the same viral code, the Revenge Virus! I wrack my brain for it, but only pieces come through.

"Doc? Dad? Anybody there?" I ask the lab.

"Yes, Jake. How can we help?" Ambrose asks.

"I need the code I created to hack Sean's computer." I hear the panic in my voice and then commotion from the lab.

"What are you doing, Jake?" Oshi asks. She stares past the

avatars with a questioning look. She knows nothing of my microchip or the lab.

"Let me through!" It's Paulie. "Jake! I have it! Your backpack's here. I have your laptop. Tell me what to do!"

I know there's way more qualified people than Paulie, but I want to give him a shot. "You can do this, Paulie. I know you can."

Meanwhile, the avatars turn a putrid shade of lime green as their bodies morph back and forth between human and gooey slugs.

"Ugh! Gross!" Oshi cries out from behind the line-up.

Raising my hands over my head, I motion to her. "Don't worry. They're not real. Just remember that."

"Ok, Jake," says Oshi, not convinced. "But what the hell is this place?"

"We're in a website."

"What the...? What are you talking about?" Still not convinced.

I say to Paulie, "Are you ready to graduate to computer literate, dude? Because you're gonna save the day."

"Hit me with it, bro," he answers.

Oshi stands with her hands on her hips goading the Gotchu gang. "Yeah, just try it. Go ahead. You don't know who you're messing with here."

Keeping my eyes glued to the gooey, green Gotchu gang, I explain to Paulie, step-by-step, how to find the Revenge Virus code in my laptop.

"I have no idea what any of it means, but it looks cool," Paulie says.

"The second you have that code I want you to send it to

my dad at the controls. I'm hoping he can electronically beam it to the chip."

"You got it," Paulie says.

Garbled, sinister laughter rings through the intersection. It's difficult to ascertain where it's coming from. Is it the programmers? Is it Stone? *Are they trying to distract me?*

Oshi continues to harass the Gotchu gang, keeping them at bay. She tries to cut through them, but they block her, touching her with their gross, gooey hands. She pushes at them, her hands sinking in. "Oooo. Disgusting! Don't touch me you vile creatures!" Each place they stroke and nudge, she turns that lime green sludge. They mob her, groping and mushing. "Get off me you repugnant monsters!" She growls at them.

I try not to sound desperate. "Paulie? I really need that code."

"Sending it to your dad now," he says, and I hear the distinct click of a keyboard and imagine he's pushing the ENTER key.

The Gotchu avatars' shapes are now morphing between green goo and code. *What the…?* Each avatar transforms into code, bright yellow streams of numbers and letters inside green, gooey globs.

This can't be good. I look past them, searching for Oshi. *Oh, no!* Oshi's almost completely metamorphosed into green goo, and yellow code flashes across her forehead. She's blending in with them.

"NO!" I scream to the lab. "They're transforming her! Give me that code!"

The Gotchu gang's original human forms are barely discernable now. They have morphed into lime green shapes filled with yellow code.

"Jake! What's happening to me?" Oshi calls out.

I close my eyes and wait for my Revenge Virus to enter my head.

CHAPTER 28
THE BATTLE FOR CODE

If there was a moment in my life where I would do anything—be stung by a thousand bees, jump off a fifty-foot-high cliff into a baby pool, have my teeth pulled out with pliers—I would do it, if it meant I could help Oshi. I focus any energy I have left into trying to remember my Revenge Virus. And then, instantaneously, the code lights up in my head.

"There you go, son," my dad says.

Without taking a millisecond to thank him, I run the code and add a few lines that will allow my virus to come alive. If I'm going to eliminate these slimy, green monsters, I need some badass avatars of my own. When I open my eyes, the physical manifestation of my Revenge Virus hovers before me—round, opalescent blue, with rotating spikes poking out it in all directions. It alternates colors as it spins: blue, purple, red, orange, green and yellow. It's beautiful, but deadly, I'm hoping.

I look towards the group of green globs surrounding Oshi. I can barely make out her features. Her body is a slimy lime green. Yellow code covers her head and one arm. Stone's programmers are draining her essence like soul-sucking fiends. Once her whole body is code, they will own her.

I close my eyes and code my virus to attack the Gotchu avatars. The luminescent ball with spikes rolls slowly, then speeds toward the circle of green globs. I target one that's reminiscent of the rapper with the floppy hat. My virus ball is a blur. Lines of brightly colored code spew from its spikes, *FWING, FWING, FWING,* pummeling the rapper. There's a sucking noise, and *POP!* Rapper avatar obliterated. A cheer from the lab.

I close my eyes and continue programming. When I open them, my virus ball is bombarding faux fur mini-skirt girl with bright fuchsia code. *Why fuchsia? Who knows?* She looks like a pink and green neon sign. And then *POP!* Another avatar eliminated.

I program my virus to attack the Gotchu gang mercilessly. Slimy blobs surround Oshi as her body slowly turns to code. *They're working hard to keep her here!* My blue virus ball pirouettes from blob to blob, like a whirling dervish, spewing vivid code from its spikes. *POP! POP!* Two more avatars burst, turning to mist.

I'm guessing the Gotchu programmers are frantically writing code at this point, trying to destroy my virus. Some of the remaining avatars are morphing between green slime and their human form as the programmers try to regain the upper hand. Suddenly, several of the avatars jolt in my direction, reanimating into their teenage characters. The kid on the skateboard speeds towards me and shoots a line of shiny, black code from a futuristic weapon. *Ha! Clever!* I leap out of the way and spin my blue ball at him. Hot, red code catapults in spitfire precision, hitting the skateboarder right between the eyes. He disappears, just like the others.

I don't have time to enjoy my victory. Who-knows-how-many programmers are involved in the fight now, with their avatars poised to attack. I've got to create more viruses to make it out of here. Luckily, I'm a faster programmer than Stone's geeks. I'm coding directly through the chip in my head, using my thoughts. I program my Revenge Virus to replicate. At once, ten viral balls are spinning around, whipping iridescent code in every direction. I focus on speeding the balls to their targets.

The tall avatar with the pink and black mohawk races toward me with a bow and arrow. *How original.* He yanks an arrow from its sheath, adjusts it in the bow and draws back the string. At the last minute he whips around and points it at Oshi!

What can I do? Instantly, I program an easy-to-remember code from *Fortress of Ninjas.* "Oshi!" I shout. Her slimy, green, yellow-coded face looks up as the ninjato sails through the air and lands at her feet. She reaches down and grabs the hilt of the Ninja sword just as Mohawk boy lets loose his arrow. Oshi rises, fast, and deftly blocks it with the flat metal sword. Meanwhile, my virus ball reaches the mohawked teenager and flings purple code at him. *POP!* He evaporates, leaving a purple haze.

Through the vapor, I see Oshi slicing at the remaining green globs closing in on her. Simultaneously, my virus balls pummel them. *POP! POP! POP!* As each one disappears, so does part of the yellow code streaming across her body. *We are winning!*

"Way to go, bro," Paulie shouts in my head. "You guys are kickin their butts!"

"Thanks," I say, clutching my head.

"Oops, sorry, dude," Paulie whispers.

It's been a long night, but I feel rejuvenated knowing Oshi is battling the avatars with me. We have annihilated most of the Gotchu gang, except for the three that stand between us now. The Gotchu coders have been busy, transforming these last three into slimy, green, gargantuan beasts. Sequined-pants girl has grown twelve feet tall with ginormous muscles. The orange-haired boy with the plaid boxers has morphed into a mountainous gooey gorilla, smashing his mighty fists into the ground, each time shaking the earth so hard it knocks me over. The girl with the black eyeliner is now a lime green ogre, spinning like a top, sending deadly, acidic goo flying in all directions. As I scramble to my feet, acidic spitballs whiz by me, burning holes wherever they land. One strikes me square on my forehead.

"Ow!" I yell. It burns like hell. *These programmers are out for blood.*

"You ok, Jake?" Dad asks.

"Yeah, yeah, I'm fine," I fib. I wipe the acid from my forehead with my sleeve and look up, hoping the enemy is watching. "We're gonna get outta here, and then I'm coming for YOU!" I shout to the gray nothingness above.

Gooey acid flings from the spinning ogre at lightning speed. We've got to put a stop to this, before Oshi and I are toast. The spitballs make a sizzling noise as they hit Oshi's sword. One gets through and hits her arm. She deftly swings round, slicing at the ogre, but the monster reaches out and slams her on the back, knocking the ninjato from her grasp. I watch in horror as she begins to turn lime green again.

The giant gorilla pounds the ground making it difficult for me to focus, but I hurtle half my viral balls at the spinning acid factory. The towering sequined-pants avatar swats at the viral balls trying to knock them off course. The ones that get through explode into thin air as they collide with the ogre's toxic goo. One survivor swirls away, then pummels the freak with constant streams of deadly, crimson code. A creepy, computer-generated *ROAR* cracks thunderously from its head. A second later I hear a giant *SLUURP!* as the ogre is sucked into a tiny green dot and *POP!* dissipates into mist.

"Whoo Hoo!" I pound my fist in the air victoriously.

Meanwhile, the programmers are overpowering Oshi. She slumps to her knees, her back covered in green slime and yellow code. I close my eyes and program a firewall to surround Oshi and protect her from further attack. *I hope!*

Suddenly, the earth shakes violently. The grotesque gorilla avatar with the colossal fists is pounding the ground—right, left, right, left—creating huge chasms, breaking the ground into chunks beneath us. I'm flung like a rag doll. I can't get my footing. *Somebody up there is having fun. Fine…I'll play.*

Despite feeling like a Mexican jumping bean, I close my eyes and program what's left of my virus balls to whirl towards the massive, slimy green gorilla. This time, I'm vicious. My viral balls don't just hurl code at him. They fly into him ferociously and imbed themselves in the green goo, releasing trails of multi-colored code inside the slime. *I've got you now!* My viruses spiral ceaselessly, burrowing themselves deeper into the gorilla as he pitches about, futilely trying to expel them. Finally, he rumbles and smashes to the ground with a thunderous *WHAM!* and then *POP!* goes the gorilla.

The balls spin in the air, waiting for my command, like happy little, *deadly*, puppies.

"Well, wasn't that special," I say out loud.

"Awesome," Paulie whispers in my head. I forgot they are there, back at the lab, watching the action.

"Jake!" Oshi calls out to me. It's obvious the enemy camp has hacked my firewall and are coding like crazy on her. The green slime is spreading down both her arms and up her neck. Everywhere it goes, yellow code soon follows.

"Impressive," I yell at them. I close my eyes and program ciphertext to confuse their code. "But it won't last!"

I feel confident that I can beat them, but then I sense impending doom. A towering presence looms over me like the shadow of death. I slowly open my eyes and look up at twelve-foot-tall sequined-pants girl holding a gigantic hair spray can six inches from my face. *Is this someone's idea of a joke?* She's got her finger on the nozzle. I squeeze my eyelids tight and program so rapidly my brain feels like it will explode.

"Look who's got you now," sequined-pants girl says, in a voice that sounds electronic and throaty. I can't battle the coders barraging Oshi *and* take out this twelve-foot-tall avatar at the same time. I'm going to need some help.

"Hey, Dad?" I ask as quietly as I can.

"I'm here," he answers pronto.

"Can you give me a hand?"

"What would you like me to do?"

Sequined-pants girl is taunting me with the spray can as Oshi continues to morph to code. I cover my mouth with my hand hoping Stone's geeks can't hear what I'm saying. "I need a stronger firewall to buy some time," I say to my dad. "I would do it myself, but I'm kinda busy here."

"Ah, but I know how you love a challenge." He chuckles. "Give me a minute."

"That's more than we can spare, Dad."

Sequined-pants girl leans back and takes aim with the giant spray can. I whirl around to avoid getting hit directly in the face. *WHOOSH!* I feel something sticky on my neck. It doesn't burn like the acid, but it smells like a cross between day-old farts, and garbage that sat in the hot sun for a week.

"What is that?" I'm freaking out.

"Oh, you'll see," she answers in a menacing electronic tone.

Suddenly, a thousand tiny spiders skitter on my neck, weaving their webs. I bat at them. The webs are expanding, wrapping themselves around me. I feel like I'm suffocating. I can't move!

"Dad! The firewall! They're trying to cut me off!"

Webs wind around my face. Stone's geeks must be onto me. They're trying to keep me from closing my eyes so I can't code. I snap them shut before the webs lock into place, keeping me from moving a muscle and making me blind to the world.

"Don't worry, Jake," my dad says as his firewall code downloads through the microchip.

I mentally force it to Oshi, and even though I can't see her, I feel confident my dad has pulled it off. Then I focus on the twelve-foot-tall avatar with a lethal can of spider spray. I must be careful. My fate is all wrapped up in this one, literally.

Since I can't open my eyes, and I have no idea where my remaining virus balls are, I rely on my intuitive perception, which is becoming highly developed. I'm able to follow sequined-pants girl's movements by the smell of the foul odor from the spray can. My viruses and I are telepathically linked now. I barely even need to code. I simply send them my thoughts and they respond. Ambrose was right—we *can* use the other 90 percent—if we believe.

My anger and frustration have reached epic proportions, so whatever spills out of me now will be a spectacle. The spider webs have paralyzed me, but there's nothing the enemy can do to stop my brain synapses from firing. *Is there?* They obviously deduced that I close my eyes to program, but do they know about the microchip? I'm praying they don't. This is my last chance to end this.

Telepathically, I transmit code to my little Frankenviruses. I hear whirring noises and then a loud, drawn-out, electronically garbled *SCREECH!* The viral balls must have hit their target because the webs loosen enough for me to squint. It's as if a rainbow nuclear bomb is exploding; fireworks of purple, red, orange, yellow, green, and blue fill my vision. The awful *SCREECHING* continues—like a dying raptor. I can't see, but I assume my viruses are destroying Sequined-Pants.

I move my mouth. It seems to be working, so I call out in a muffled voice, "Oshi? You there?" No response. As the webs relax I open my eyes a bit further and try to locate her. A kaleidoscopic mist veils my vision. Then I hear a faint "I'm okay" off in the distance.

As the webs finally release, I fall to my knees, gagging. I pluck at the sticky threads, pulling them from my face and stretching them off my body. Blinking furiously, I try raising my eyelids. Finally, while the colorful clouds disperse, I glimpse my viruses literally feeding on Sequined-Pants like little Pac-Mans. In one of my last transmissions, I gave them gaping mouths, with super sharp, pointy teeth and big appetites for twelve-foot tall avatar monster girls. She heaves one last *SCREECH* as the viruses devour her. And then…*POP!* A lightshow fills the intersection as the last avatar is annihilated. The ominous spray can with the foul smell hits the pavement. Hundreds of tiny, immobile, metallic spiders litter the street. *Clever programming, I'll give them that.*

"They can't code fast enough to hit me again right now," I think. We've destroyed all their avatars. I imagine whatever stamina they have left is being poured into cracking my dad's firewall. *All hands on deck, so to speak.*

The multi-colored nuclear fallout is fading, and I pat myself to confirm I'm okay. Oshi stands in the same spot, half numbers, half human, protected by a force field of impenetrable code. She puts her green, yellow-coded arms up in the universal sign for *WTF?*

"Okay, Dad…" I'm going to tell him to release the firewall, when I'm slammed to the ground. The most colossal pain I've ever felt in my life is boring a hole through my brain.

A familiar voice says, "Well, hello there, Jake…uh…that's Jake *Green*, am I right?"

It's Buckminster Stone.

CHAPTER 29
MEETING OF THE MASTERMINDS

I clutch my skull. Stone's voice fills my head. "Seems like you've got a little chippy implant, don't you?" Stone taunts. He's hacked into the microchip. It feels like a bulldozer is excavating my brain.

"Owwwww..." I scream. A thousand firecrackers are exploding in my head. I roll up into a pathetic little ball on the asphalt, moaning and crying.

"It's simply mind-boggling how easily these technologies are hacked and manipulated ...at least...by the right individual," he says with a note of self-aggrandizement.

I rock myself in the fetal position. "What...do...you... want?" I eke out.

"This is all an experiment, dear boy," he answers in a much softer tone, like he's trying to calm a group of small children. "Haven't you figured that out yet? And your friend here ... Oshi?...she's a major player in it now, because you effectively eliminated any other prospects by intercepting my virus."

"It...was...an...accident."

"Yes, yes," he says dismissively. "And, here you are, disrupting the experiment again. Hundreds, if not thousands, of people would have clicked on the Gotchu box, and been transported here." Stone pauses as if in thought, then his tone becomes more acerbic. "But thanks to your jealous fit, we are left with only one subject—your friend over there." He practically spits this last out. "It's a small price to pay, don't you think, Jake?"

"Please! I can't think," I beg.

"Oh, all right." Stone releases a fraction of the control over my microchip. The pain subsides to a burning pulse every time I move a fraction of an inch. I grimace and glance over at Oshi, still half code, half human. She tries to move toward me, but the programmers have her pinned. Undoubtedly, they are working furiously to crack my dad's firewall. *Good luck!* As if Stone can read my mind he says, "Forget about your friend. We have her. End of story."

"You. Are. Evil." I spew out the words.

"Oh, I wouldn't go that far, Jake," Stone says, his voice calm again. "Perhaps some people think so, but I have a very Earth-friendly agenda. My plan may take years to perfect, but we can't get anywhere without human test subjects. You see, the planet is dying because it is simply overrun with *homo sapiens*. If 80 percent of them, or even half of them, could live out their lives here, within the Web, wouldn't that alleviate some of the problems we're facing on this endangered planet of ours?"

As Stone engages with me, he eases up on my microchip, and the pain lessens. I realize I must keep him engaged. I slowly sit up, holding back nausea as the world spins. My clothes are soaked in sweat. "Oh, and you're the *god* that's going to choose who goes, and who stays, in the real world?"

Stone chuckles impatiently, as if I'm a silly little boy who doesn't understand big concepts. "You've got me all wrong, Jake. I'm no god, simply a humble scientist trying to save the world from imminent destruction. Tim Berners-Lee developed the World Wide Web for all of humanity. In the interest of saving humanity, I'm simply taking it to the next level. Oh, and by the way, if you're wondering why your father, or Ambrose, isn't coming to your defense, it's because I have hacked their system and blocked access. They aren't privy to this conversation."

"What do you want? A geek medal?"

Stone laughs. "No need to be snarky, young man," he says. "What I really want is for you to realize that it's too late for your friend. She must remain here, so that we may continue with our experiment."

Stone notices the look of horror and disgust on my face. "It's not like she'll be dead! You could even join her, if you like, although I doubt your acclaimed father would like that."

"What do you know about my father." I say tersely, keeping Stone occupied. Meanwhile, I'm hoping my dad and Ambrose are reverse-engineering Stone's hack and restoring the system. As long as Stone is in my head though, I won't be able to talk with them. If I close my eyes to concentrate, Stone will know I'm programming, and ratchet up the pain. I'm totally on my own.

My viruses munched through their prize and now they loll about, like triumphant little furballs, waiting for direction. Stone hacked my microchip, but he obviously hasn't cracked the code for my viruses, or they would have disappeared by now. I must reach them telepathically, without alerting Stone.

"What's your problem with my dad, anyway?" I ask him.

"We had fundamentally different points of view on what

the ENERGENX PROJECT should accomplish, that's all," he answers.

Conversing with Stone, while transmitting code to my viruses, is like patting my head and rubbing my belly, but I need to keep him engaged. "Like what?" I ask.

"Your father," Stone says, "and that featherbrained Ambrose..." he huffs... "did not see my vision. They were against sending those fellows into the Web. Well, to be fair, the Web was in its infancy then. Scientists used it to share information mostly. None of us knew exactly what would happen, but we had protocols in place for every possible outcome...at least...we thought we did."

Keep talking you demonic, crazy, whack-job. "Uh, huh...," I say. I concentrate to speak because what I'm really focusing on is transmitting code to my viruses.

"But what happened?" I ask Stone. "Why didn't those guys rematerialize?"

A long silence ensues, during which time I'm able to formulate my plan. Finally, Stone answers, "Well, I don't really know. This is what I have spent the last twenty-five years and millions of dollars to discover. Technological advances have given me the means to develop what I think is a far superior transmutation method. If you decide to come with us, Jake, I will share it with you, if you like."

Focus, Jake, focus. He's waiting for a response. I stutter, "Uh, yeah, yeah...I'll think about it."

"I assume you have devised a plan for returning to the *real world*, as you call it," he says.

I don't answer immediately. My mind is in a trance, but I realize I'm going to be discovered if I don't respond. "Yeah, we've got a plan," I manage, but Stone notices that I'm hedging. I should have known he's too smart not to catch on. I must make my move now, before he burns my brain to a crisp.

"Jake...Jake...Jake," he says slowly. "What are you up to?"

And I know this is it.

In the split second it will take Stone to dial up the pain, I put my plan into action. A viral ball sends a rapid blast of code to my microchip, disabling it, so I am cut off completely from the lab, *and* Stone's control. He's no longer in my head, but neither is my dad, Ambrose, or Paulie. For the first time since I entered the Gotchu website, I'm sure I won't make it back.

CHAPTER 30
A WAY OUT

It's quiet, deadly quiet. The sound loops stop, and the noise of battle is over. I think I've freaked everybody out, in both camps. Stone thinks he's got me, and my dad thinks he's lost me. I look across the empty intersection and there stands Oshi—the top half of her body flickering yellow code on a green tinted background, like a lonely neon sign in the night.

Is the firewall still up? It's hard to say. Without my microchip, I'm not sure about anything. A dull ache is all that remains of the shattering pain Stone planted in my head. I push myself off the ground and fall back down again. I'm weak. I force myself to stand and trudge on rubbery legs to Oshi.

It's strange seeing my best friend outfitted in luminescent code. It's like staring at a blinking florescent light that's losing its juice. Oshi's scratchy voice drops in and out like a remote radio station. "I hope...have a plan...getting us...of here."

"I'm working on it," I reassure her. But the truth is, I'm fresh out of ideas. Stone has a stable of programmers madly coding to control Oshi. I take one of her twinkling hands and hold it in both of mine. It feels fantastic to finally touch her, even though she's a bit doughy and code streams across her hand. If we're stuck in this website forever, at least we'll be together. Undulating numbers flutter across her face, but I can still feel her eyes searching mine.

"What's hap...to me?" she asks in that same static voice.

"I will explain everything, I promise, but first we need to get out of here."

We stand side-by-side, holding hands, just like we used to when my dad sprayed us with the hose on a hot summer day. She lays her head on my shoulder. We stay that way for what seems like a long time but is probably only a few minutes, and suddenly I'm back in my aching body, painfully aware of our circumstances. My mind races. I need to communicate with the lab badly, and soon. It's only a matter of time before Stone breaks through my dad's firewall and overtakes Oshi... for good. *Yeah, that's not happening!*

I place my hands on Oshi's gelatinous shoulders. "I have an idea." I leave her protected by the firewall. Crossing the intersection, I wrack my brain thinking of some way to send a signal to the lab. I need an electronic source, something I can use to make a transmitter. I remind myself that this is a fabricated world, created for Stone's twisted experiment. A world in which he is trying to make Oshi and me permanent residents. My mind floods with panicky thoughts: *What about our families? What do we eat? Where do we sleep? What about school?* I shake my head. *STOP! Focus!*

I pace circles around the area. It's eerily quiet. *Come on, Jake!* And then I notice it—the stoplights are still flashing red to yellow and back again. I run over to the pole and climb it, not letting myself think about how dangerous this is. The programmers could catch me any moment and *disappear* the pole.

Luckily, it isn't too high, maybe fifteen feet. In my current condition, I'm struggling, and not finding any electrical wiring as I inch up the pole. This isn't a good sign. I reach the top. The stoplight is housed in a metal box. It's placed clumsily on the top of the pole. I lift it off carefully to check for anything I can use, but it slips from my fingers and *crashes* to the ground making a loud CRUNCHING noise. I pray my connection to Stone's programmers is as severed as it is to the lab.

I wait, unmoving, for something to happen, but when nothing does, I slide down quickly and examine the battered bits of plastic and metal on the ground. Hidden among them is a small transponder, an electrical unit programmed to control the lights.

Now what? What can I do without the microchip?

All that's left is my capacity to use the other 90 percent of my brain. I sit down on the asphalt, close my eyes, and communicate telepathically with my viruses. Holding the transponder in my palms, I breathe slowly and concentrate. I feel the rush of the viruses whirling around me. This could be dangerous, but I need the combined energy of my brain and my viruses to power the transponder. I open my palms and force one spinning virus perilously close. The transponder begins to vibrate, ever so slightly. I break my concentration for a millisecond to check on Oshi. The transponder becomes still. Squinting through an aqua cloud created by the virus balls, I'm comforted to see that Oshi's body remains intact, code streaming across it, but no more body parts morphing. I smile at her. She nods.

I close my eyes and focus. The little transponder begins to vibrate again. I plan to utilize its tech to reach the lab through my mind. *This is insane. What am I doing?* I place myself in the lab; smell the aromas, see the technicians at their monitors, hear my dad and Ambrose. *Focus. Focus.* Nothing happens. My palms are sweaty. The transponder is growing warmer. I block all other thoughts and focus on the lab. *Come on, Jake, concentrate.*

Suddenly, there is a voice in my head. "Jake?"

"Dad?" I answer back with my mind. *This is unbelievable. I've done it. I'm telepathically communicating with the lab!*

"Yes, son. Hang on for just a second. Ambrose and the team…they…"

And then, loudly, through the Gotchu speakers: "Jake!"

"Ambrose?" It sounds like he's in an echo chamber, his voice coming from all directions.

"It is I!" He exclaims. "We were able to reverse-engineer Stone's hack. We have complete control of the website now. We lost you. What's going on there?"

I'm astounded this is all happening at once—my newly discovered psychokinetic skills, and the lab's ability to decompile Stone's hack. I answer Ambrose. "Stone took control of the microchip and got inside my head." *He almost killed me.* "I had to disable the microchip to stop him."

"And Oshi?" he asks.

"She's half code and the Gotchu programmers are trying to finish her off…keep her here…I don't know. Stone wants to keep us both here."

"Well, that's not happening," Dad says. "We're bringing you back now."

"Fantastic, Dad! But…Oshi…" I run over to her, as if to make the point that I'm not going anywhere without her. She takes my hand.

"Don't worry, Jake," Ambrose says. "We have the programmers blocked for the present moment. Now, stand back."

I let go of Oshi's hand and step aside. Slowly, working from the middle of her body to the top of her head, the programmers' code is deleted, and Oshi's human form is reappearing. I hold my breath until the last character is erased. I grab Oshi's hand.

"Thank you, doc," I breathe.

"You can thank your father, Jake. He's the one stroking the keyboard."

"You're my hero, Dad," I say.

"Yes, thank you so much!" Oshi adds. "Now, can we please get out of here?"

"Yes! We need to get you both back here immediately," my dad responds. "Those programmers are working frantically to undermine us."

"Ok, Dad. We're ready when you are."

I keep Oshi close, ready for transmutation. "Don't worry," I tell her. "It'll be fun. Just like the rides at the fair."

"Here goes," my dad says, and suddenly I feel that same tingling I felt in the pod. Our bodies are encircled by the same kinetic kaleidoscope of colors, spinning faster and faster. Oshi looks at me for reassurance. I hold her tightly.

Oshi squirms. "Whoa! Wha…what's happening?" She shrieks.

I smile at her. "This is a million times better than the carnival, and it'll be super quick. Enjoy the trip!" Swiftly, our bodies transmute into billions of colorful swirling pinpoints and I black out, again.

CHAPTER 31
THE REAL WORLD

As my body reintegrates from energetic to solid, I realize that Oshi and I are squished together in an uncomfortable posture—legs and arms akimbo, crossing over and under each other.

With a *whoosh*, the pod door swings open, and we untangle and stumble out into my dad's grasp. "Have a seat," he says. Lab assistants guide us into chairs. My muscles are weak, and my brain is fried. Oshi's eyes are bulbous and red-lined, like her circuits are frayed. We're readjusting to the energy here in the real world.

Sara pushes bottles of Gatorade into our hands, "Drink. You need electrolytes," she says. It tastes so good I guzzle the whole bottle. Oshi places the cool plastic against her cheeks.

Ambrose leans on some equipment nearby, watching us, looking as exhausted as we are. "We did it," he says.

"We did it," I agree. My mind whirls as I reflect on what we all just went through. I turn to Oshi, "Are you okay?"

She nods and takes a sip of her Gatorade, then adds quietly, "What. A. Rush."

Paulie twirls around. "Whoo hoo! You guys rock! I want to go in the pod!"

"Not happening any time soon, son." Ambrose tells Paulie. "Too stressful." He smiles knowingly at me, then begins to pace slowly. "But what a remarkably successful experiment, no? You were transmuted and you returned, unharmed. A miracle. Too bad we cannot report it or recount it to *anyone*."

"This experience remains here," I say.

"My lips are sealed," Paulie says, imitating a zipper across his lips.

"Sara?"

Sara covers her mouth with her hands.

"Not even Mumsy?" I ask.

"Not even Mumsy," she confirms.

I catch my father's eyes. "I've kept this technology secret for almost thirty years, son. I think I can go another thirty," he says.

I search the faces of Ambrose's trusted assistants. "Don't worry about them, Jake," Ambrose assures me. "They are used to discretion." The technicians nod. "Otherwise, they won't get their dissertations approved." Ambrose chuckles. "Besides, who would believe any of this anyway?" He looks at his assistants through furrowed brows, and then pointedly at me. "Not to mention, this technology could be dangerous in the wrong hands."

Dad steps in front of me. "Well, you are both safe, that's what matters." He raises his arms for a hug. I rise unsteadily and fall into them. Sara tumbles into us. "Whoa!" Dad yelps, steadying us. I motion to Paulie and Oshi to join our tenuous house of cards.

It's difficult leaving the contented warmth of this group hug, but I extricate myself and shuffle towards Ambrose. He's talking with one of his assistants, his back to me. I tap him on the shoulder. "Thanks for everything, Ambrose. I...we... couldn't have done this without your help, and the help of your staff." I wave at his assistants. They nod.

"Do not trouble yourself, Jake," Ambrose says. "How could I refuse? Your situation was a compelling one." Ambrose lays a hand on my shoulder and leans in closer. "Plus, I got to use the pod." He winks and pats me on the back. "Now, go get some much deserved rest!" He turns to his assistant again. As I walk away he adds, "Plus, Stone's plans must be...*disrupted*... no?"

I stop, the full weight of his words washing over me. I look back at Ambrose. He bobs his head at me, one time, in a show of mutual respect and understanding.

I'm brought back to the room by a slap on the back. "Way to go, dude! This whole thing is so frakkin awesome!" Paulie proclaims excitedly.

"I couldn't have done it without you," I say truthfully.

"Dude, this has been the most kick-ass three days of my life. I don't know how I'm going to go back to my boring existence." He punches an invisible boxing bag. "My parental units will be here any minute to pick me up, and man, are they pissed."

"I'm sorry," I say.

"No worries, bro. They didn't realize I was gone until your dad called them in the wee hours. I'm on restriction for, like, a hundred years, plus, they'll probably send me to another school to avoid contact with you, but that won't keep me away." He lifts his palm for a high five. I slap his hand and we pound knuckles.

"Come on, Paulie," Dad calls. "Your folks are outside. I'll walk you out and contrive something that makes sense for them. Perhaps an experiment you were helping Jake with? You too, Sara. Your mom is here."

"Am I in trouble?" Sara asks.

Dad shrugs, "She's not happy, that's for sure, but maybe I can help." He squeezes my shoulder. "I can give you and Oshi a ride home if you like."

"Okay, Dad," I say, feeling grateful. "And thanks for dealing with Mumsy."

Dad ushers Sara and Paulie out the back entrance, and I hobble to where Oshi is resting. Her hair is tousled, and her eyelids are heavy. Even though I'm relieved to finally be safe and alone together, my stomach feels tangled in knots. My jealousy played a role in this fiasco. It's time to come clean. I turn my chair to face her.

"Oshi? I... I haven't been honest with you," I hesitate. Underneath the bruises and dirt, I'm sure my face is the color of beets. "I want to be your boyfriend. Not Sean."

Oshi rouses and sits up. "Wh…what?"

"Yeah," I fumble, searching for the right words to tell her how I feel. Feelings I've held back for so long, they gush out like a tsunami. "I didn't know until recently…and…believe me, it's the last thing I wanted…," I try to clarify. "I mean, it's the last thing I expected. I didn't want to ruin our friendship—especially that—so I didn't tell you. It's been awful. I feel like such an idiot."

An awkward silence seems to go on for days. *Come on, say something, Oshi! I'm drowning.* Instead, she reaches out and takes my hand. My cheeks burn and my heart pounds against my chest so hard I'm certain she can see it.

Oshi looks into my eyes and I feel like she's boring into my soul, trying to read me. *Why are girls so good at this stuff?* I feel like my skin is about to crinkle and fall off. I can't read Oshi's thoughts, even with my newfound superpowers.

"This a new development," she says finally, and I breathe again. She continues, "I just need...time. It's all been...overwhelming."

"Yeah, yeah, I get it," I say, much too quickly, gushing again, feeling bad for even bringing this up on top of everything else she's been through. "I just...wanted you to know, ya know, how I'm feeling."

"Explains a lot," she smiles and lets go of my hand.

We both flop back in our chairs, fatigue setting in. Oshi's eyelids droop and finally close, but I don't know if I will ever be able to close my eyelids again. Battling Stone will be etched there forever.

Twenty minutes later, Oshi and I are sitting in the back of Dad's old Volvo fabricating a story to tell her parents.

"I'm scared, Jake," Oshi says. "I can't believe I was gone for so long. What am I supposed to tell them?"

"You decided to go check out colleges?" I offer.

She laughs out loud. "That's something you normally do with your parents."

"Okay, seriously, we ought to be able to come up with something," I say.

"It'd better be convincing, and soon, we're almost there," she laments.

We take an exit and drive through serene neighborhoods. Ribbons of prismatic early morning light shine through the trees. A pudgy, middle-aged man in a bathrobe grabs his newspaper off the lawn, and a fit, young woman in Spandex jogs past.

"I think I've got it," I say.

"Okay." Oshi waits.

"I kidnapped you."

Dad looks in the rearview. I wave a hand at him.

Oshi interrupts. "But that makes no sense, Jake. You were asking everybody about me. Aunt June? Sean? My friends? Why would you do that if you knew where I was?"

"As a cover?"

"No one is going to believe that you're suddenly a psychopath, Jake," she says. "Besides, everyone knows you love me." She blushes. I blush. Dad glances at us.

"I may be able to help here," Dad says. "What if you were working on a really important project and I was mentoring you?"

"I don't know, Dad," I say. "There's a lot of holes in that explanation."

"Well, I'm already known for being a bit...nuts. Maybe I just forgot how long you were at my place," He offers.

"I got this," Oshi says. "I told Aunt June I was staying at a friend's. I'll call Angie and ask her to cover for me."

"And why didn't you call Aunt June for two days?" I ask.

"I...uh...I don't know. I forgot?" Oshi lamely answers.

"Big hole, but okay, I guess," I don't sound convincing.

"I'll cover for you," Dad offers. "Yeah...I was helping you with a project."

"That's why I wasn't at school," Oshi offers.

"Yes," I pipe in. "You were at the lab with Ambrose. My dad introduced you. That's how you ended up there. Say you think you've figured out time travel. They'll think you're bonkers." I pause. "You may have to go to therapy."

Silence. We all know it's the longest stretch on the planet.

Oshi shakes her head. "I'm going to be in a shit-ton of trouble."

I put my arm around Oshi for the last few minutes of the drive. "You can do this," I tell her. She doesn't look persuaded, and I'm not sure this whole thing won't blow up.

"Don't worry. Dad and I will get the story straight and call Ambrose. You better call Angie right away. Your parents are gonna be super pissed, for sure." I'm terrified for Oshi. Bile rises in my esophagus. I swallow it down.

We are a few blocks from Oshi's house. We stare at each other, the reality of what we're about to do sinking in. The sunshine through the window casts a radiant light on her face. It's the most beautiful thing I've ever seen. It isn't the first time, and I'm sure it won't be the last time, Oshi O'Malley makes my heart leap.

I extricate a piece of greenish colored spider web from her hair. "Um…Oshi?" I begin.

Suddenly she hugs me. A bear couldn't hug tighter. I can feel the blood rush to my face. When she releases me, she looks at me with those big, brown eyes as if she'll never see me again. A tear spills down her cheek.

I gently wipe the tear away. "I love you," I say.

"I love you too, Jake Green." Oshi's lips briefly touch mine.

"We're here, kids," Dad says as we pull up to the curb.

Noooooooo! I'm not ready to say goodbye. I may never see her again.

Oshi's parents are waiting on the porch. My gut clenches at the thought of what this uncertain future holds.

Oshi turns to me. "I'll text you," she says, like it's any old day.

"Now, get out of here before you have to talk to my parents." She jumps out of the car and trudges towards the porch. The anguish covering her enchanting features breaks my heart.

"Let's go, Dad" I beckon him. Oshi's eyes search for me as her parents hug her tightly, then raise their arms in exasperation. As we drive away I hear them: *Where were you? The police are looking for you. We were worried sick! We flew all the way home from Japan!*

"Bye Jake!" Oshi yells, as her parents escort her into the house, away from me, maybe forever.

EPILOGUE—TWO WEEKS LATER

Dad knocks on my bedroom door. "Dinner's ready." I set my laptop aside and scramble to the kitchen. I'm starved.

Mumsy and Sara set dishes and napkins on the table. It feels like old times, but it's not. Dad hasn't moved back in, and I don't believe he ever will, especially after this last stunt. Mumsy doesn't understand why Oshi wouldn't text me for three whole days. I had to explain to her my newfound feelings for Oshi, and my jealousy over her relationship with Sean Haggerty. That softened things a bit.

Still, Mumsy's angry that I lied to her and dragged Sara into the whole thing. Sara's been a trooper though, keeping up with the story that we were out looking for Oshi, and found her at the lab with Dad.

I haven't heard from Paulie nor have I seen him around, so I guess his parents did follow through on changing schools. They must have taken his phone away too, otherwise he'd text me, I'm sure of it. I keep expecting him to show up behind the garbage cans.

I see Oshi at school, but she's been forbidden to talk to me, and her parents have spies reporting to them. To keep the peace, I don't approach her, and since I'm not allowed in the computer lab, I don't run into her there. She had to switch lockers, which is especially heartbreaking, but I trust that we'll be back together, after all this settles. It might be, like, when we're in our twenties, but I know it will happen. I'm just grateful she's home safe.

I feel like I've been to hell and back, still, everything seems peaceful and homey tonight, and that's alright with me. We sit down and dive into the big pot of Mumsy's famous spaghetti.

Halfway through dinner Dad says, "I heard from your mother that Dr. Lavinski has offered you a job at the lab this summer. Is that true?"

I nod.

"Hmmm," he starts. "Well, Jake, that's quite an accomplishment. I'm sure you'll be the youngest lab assistant there."

"Yeah, probably," I say. "But I'm okay with that. I'll get to learn a lot and Ambrose says that some of those students could learn a thing or two from my computing skills."

Mumsy chimes in. "Yes, and you'll be putting those skills to positive use, rather than using them to hack into innocent people's computers."

"Mom," I say. "I only did that for experience. I wasn't going to continue."

She eyes me sideways, a forkful of noodles about to enter her mouth.

"Good," Dad says. "But that lab is experimenting with some very cutting-edge technology, and..."

Sara and I give him the evil eye, reminding him not to mention what goes on in the lab.

Mumsy becomes suspicious. "Why? What goes on there?"

I adopt my casual demeanor. "Nothing, Mumsy. Dad's just concerned because they use a few toxic chemicals. It's no big deal, really."

"Yeah," Sara echoes enthusiastically. "No big deal at all."

I squeeze Sara's knee under the table. Her eyes bug out, but Mumsy doesn't notice.

"Well, that was delicious, even if I do say so myself." Mumsy pushes her chair back and takes her plate to the sink. I lean over to my dad and whisper, "It's okay, Dad, don't worry. I'm just going to assist Ambrose in his day-to-day activities, you know, normal stuff that goes on in a research lab."

"But it's not normal, is it? It's a *paranormal* research lab," he emphasizes. "Be careful, Jake."

"I promise," I say. But I'm thinking about that 90 percent and how I want to access more of it. I stand up. "I need to get back to my homework." I give him a quick hug. Mumsy comes back to the table. "My, my...aren't we affectionate this evening. I don't know what's come over you, but I like it." She smiles.

I wave her off. "I'm outta here."

I make sure the Keep Out sign is secure as I shut my bedroom door. Leaning back on propped pillows, I flip open my laptop. The browser window opens to a saved article in the technology section of the *San Francisco Chronicle*. The headline reads:

Computer Technology Guru Establishes
Foundation to Research Overpopulation

Below the headline is a picture of Buckminster Stone, grinning from ear to ear. Behind him stands a cadre of young men and women, probably the very same programmers that tried to kidnap me and Oshi.

I open another tab at the top of my screen. A page of code appears. I've been working on it all week: a formidable viral code for a special person who thinks he can escape the clutches of justice. I've created it especially for the website of the **Stone Foundation for Overpopulation Research**. Stone won't know what hit him, until it's too late.

ACKNOWLEDGMENTS

Jake/Geek would not have been written and published without help from the following all-stars:

Deborah Vetter, my instructor at The Institute for Writers, who ushered me through the process of writing my first novel for teens with the expertise of her long-time career as Executive Editor of *Cricket* and *Cicada* magazines and Senior Contributing Editor at Cricket Books. It's been a while, Debby, but I'm eternally grateful.

Martha Bullen of Bullen Publishing Services, whose proficiency in the publishing arena is unparalleled. Thanks for your unwavering patience and guidance in bringing *Jake/Geek* to the finish line.

Gareth Carter, techno-wizard in London, who assisted in guaranteeing that I got all the technology bits right.

Christy Collins of Constellation Book Services, who steered me through uncharted waters with her friendly manner, book design skills and steadfastness. She and her team got me from uncertain how to proceed to holding a copy of *Jake/Geek* in my hands.

Chinthaka Pradeep for the *Jake/Geek* cover art. Chinthaka's ability to listen to my ideas with patience, and translate them into the perfect illustration, was spellbinding. You can find Chinthaka as Bee Creations on Fiverr.com.

Riley Haslett, my daughter, who patiently listens (and listens, and listens) to rewrites and ideas, and who was instrumental in deciding on the cover art. I love you, honey. Thanks for all your input.

A myriad of family and friends who were with me all the way— reading the book, giving me feedback, and generally just cheering me on. They know my story and what I went through during the ten years it took to get *Jake/Geek* from an idea to a finished book. At the risk of leaving someone out accidentally, I'll just say, YOU KNOW WHO YOU ARE, and I love you.

Finally, a special word for my beloved husband, L. Hawk Cargo, who is in the ethers now. Even though you didn't really "get" this sci-fi story about a teenage hacker, you were always supportive of my dreams. I miss you.

ABOUT THE AUTHOR

REONNE HASLETT has an immense imagination. As early as age seven, she orchestrated the neighborhood kids' playtime from her time machine (a refrigerator box). Being chased by dinosaurs or piloting a rocket of space explorers was her daily routine. Once she picked up a pencil, she couldn't stop. By the 3rd grade her stories were winning awards.

She has been writing professionally her entire adult life. Due to her natural curiosity, she has a passion for science fiction and the supernatural. Her love of storytelling led her to the film business, where she wrote and edited screenplays as well as produced feature films, including *Quest of the Delta Knights*, a 15th century fantasy. Reonne continues to express her vivid ideas on the page with her debut sci-fi/fantasy novel for young adults, *Jake/Geek*.

Her current projects are a YA supernatural thriller involving some creatures no one has yet put a name to, and a TV pilot blending the paranormal with the mining history of her home town, Grass Valley, California. She lives among the evergreens with her old tabby cat. To learn more about Reonne and *Jake/Geek*, please visit www.reonnehaslett.com.